Winter Quarters

William Mayne

PUFFIN BOOKS

To Kaye Webb

Puffin Books, Penguin Books Ltd, Harmondsworth, Middlesex, England
Viking Penguin Inc, 40 West 23rd Street, New York, New York 10010, U.S.A.
Penguin Books Australia Ltd, Ringwood, Victoria, Australia
Penguin Books Canada Ltd, 2801 John Street, Markham, Ontario, Canada L3R 1B4
Penguin Books (N.Z.) Ltd, 182–190 Wairau Road, Auckland 10, New Zealand

First published by Jonathan Cape Ltd 1982
Published in Puffin Books 1984

Made and printed in Great Britain by
Richard Clay (The Chaucer Press) Ltd,
Bungay, Suffolk
Set in VIP Meridien

Contents

1

No Entry

Lall was sitting in the back of a covered lorry going slowly along a country road. She was hidden by the contents of the lorry, in the twilight under the tilt. She was looking after the dark baby of her sister Beverley, talking to it, hearing it, seeing its bright brown eyes show all that went into them.

The lorry was pulling a caravan, or living-trailer. Lall could see its front window following closely all the time, with its lace curtains swaying. In it was a reflection of the back of the lorry she was in, a dark hump, and round that a view of the passing countryside, running to the edge of the diamond panes, to turn actual and vanish, taking real trees, poles and buildings, with it; printing the world and destroying it at the same time. A similar shrinking, moving view went into the baby's shining eyes.

Lall could see right through the trailer, through the back window, to what was following, a steam traction engine, black and gold, its own trailer behind it, red and gold. Occasionally she smelt steam and smoke. Her lorry, blue and crimson, was going slowly to keep the traction engine company. Ahead were two more lorries with trailers, a car towing a box of freight, and the grey-green motor bike of Laban Gozzle. Behind the traction engine was a fully-laden wagon with a long trailer, both many-coloured like the Big Wheel they carried. Last was a light truck, ready to give a push or a pull on hills. It was grey-green, painted from the same pot as the motor bike, its tilt the same canvas as the panniers of the bike.

The long train of vehicles was called the coffle. It had been going since the beginning of daylight, and the time was slow and the world was cold. Lall was sitting in a hard place, bone against bone, and there was nowhere else to go. The baby was on a cot mattress, was wrapped in a shawl, and was firmly dressed under that. It rode soft and stiff, like a shell on a cushion.

Both of them were on a floor that was turned face down, all ribs and roughness, and were under the head of a wood and plaster duck, with a red throat that the paint was wearing away from. Between Lall's knees was the stalk the duck stood on, when it whirled round not very fast on its carousel, or merry-go-round. Now it was having a ride itself, and Lall sat under it. The duck stood calmly on its stalk, not knowing anything better. Its big blue eye, quite unnatural, looked at the canvas sides of the lorry, reflecting nothing; nothing came in, nothing went out. Its eyelashes needed new paint.

Lall's name was a difficult one. What she could be called depended on who was speaking to her. If she wrote it down she would write Lall, all she would put on paper. But there was more. Anybody could call her Lall. It was not a Christian name, or forename, or surname or family name. Anyone could know that name, and use it, because things have names.

Her next name she would write if she had to, and people thought it was her surname, but it was more private than that: it was the name her mother called her, Routh, to rhyme with mouth. Her family would use that name; her close friends might. Her mother's name was Jane Ellerby, and something else. The world called her Jane, but Lall called her Ellerby.

All of them among Lall's people had names like that. Each had, too, the third name, never written down, never told, and which would only be used two or three times in their lives: when they were given names after being born, when they took a husband or wife, and on one or two other special occasions.

The baby had no name yet, nothing at all; but Lall thought its familiar name would be Rise, where it had been born. Since she was its aunt, and washed and dressed it, she knew it was a boy; but the customs of the people were clear: so far it was an it; when the time came the sex would be decided, or made clear, and names given. Now it flashed its landscaped eyes and made happy bubblings, nameless.

So Lall for ordinary, Lall eleven years ordinary, sat hard in the bottom of a lorry and was taken through the clouded skies of the countryside, on the way to their winter quarters.

The train of vehicles was for living and working in. Lall and the baby sat under part of the work now. In the coffle were the hoop-la and rifle range, where you could win enormous cuddly toys, in the first wagon; in the second a darts booth, where you could win silvery things, and a small train ride for little children; in Lall's the roundabout; and in the back wagon of the coffle the Big Wheel, the ride you found false teeth under at the end of the day. It was run by Nazar Wawne and Fahkri, the baby's father, when he was here. The steam engine drove all at each gaff, or fairground.

Now work was over for the year, and the coffle was going to winter quarters at Burton, between the mere and the sea. The coffle went slowly along, or trees and telegraph poles went slowly by. Now and then a message went along the line, a hooting of horns, and a shriek or two from the steam engine.

It would have been warmer in the engine, Lall thought, warmer but coaly. Last year she had ridden in the engine, but it had rained, so she had got cold and wet one side, and hot and dirty on the other. The baby would have liked being on the tender.

The view dropped away to one side, opening out, as if the trailer side had fallen off. In fact the coffle was passing the mere, the lake it spent the winter by.

Lall got up from her place under the duck, banged her head on its rump, cracked her knee on a trestle, and untangled her way through the load until she came to the back.

"Good baby," she said. "Lall go lookies."

The mere was on the right of the road. Today it was unpainted, the colour of metal, dull but rippled with a cold wind. The trees beyond it stood gold and brown, and were reflected as a muddy stain.

That was the first look at the mere. Then trees came between the road and the water, and the water did not have enough light to send through the leaves and branches and be seen.

Houses began, at first beyond hedges and grassy banks, then with names beyond walls, and then beyond pavements and sidewalks, with numbers, not names. "Housey people live here," she told the baby. "All the time."

A little while after that there were houses beyond houses, other roads beyond the one the coffle was in. The other roads came to meet that road, and traffic waited for them to pass.

The lorry went slower and slower. The trailer behind

nodded less and less. Its window filled up with windows of houses, with passing buses, with gables and standing sky. It nodded its last, and they were all at a standstill. There was a plaintive cry from the steam engine, and it halted with the front of its boiler close against the back of the trailer. It was so close that Lall could see smoke rising over the trailer.

A motorist in a side street peeped his horn at Lall's lorry and trailer, which lay across his path. Lall looked at him; he looked at her. He had a moustache. He turned his Land Rover and went another way when the road remained blocked. Lall knew him; she knew his greenish moustache. He was a farmer, but not a friendly one. All the same, seeing him meant that she was back on familiar ground. She felt a twitch of excitement at the thought of settling for the winter.

On the other side of the road Laban Gozzle's grey-dun motor bike came thudding up, Laban astride the striving thing like a child outrider, his face tiny inside the army helmet. He was saying words as he went by. Lall knew he must be swearing, because there was no one to speak to, and no one could hear. Laban paused at the steam engine, speaking to Lavender, the driver, then went on along the line of the coffle. Lall could hear the motor banging further and further away.

Laban came scorching down the road again, against the traffic, getting shouted at in turn. Everything had stopped moving either way along the road. The coffle was close to the end of its journey but not yet at it. Lall knew where she was. She thought it was right that everything should stop for them when they came to town, but not likely things had stopped willingly. She set out to discover why. She went back under the tilt of the lorry for the baby, picking it up in its blanket, rigid like a sturdy plant in a pot, climbed out with it, and stood in the road. There was road both sides of the lorry. She walked back to the steam engine and climbed up the side of the coalbox to Lavender. "What for have we stopped?" she asked.

"Can't get in our field," said Lavender. "Gate's shut, locked, fast, chained, nailed, posted, guarded. They don't want us in."

"Don't be daft," said Lall. "They can't keep us out of our spot."

"Don't reckon on it," said Lavender. "We expected it a bit. He kind of said, last time. It's got like that all over, you can't stop and live, you don't get allowed. What do they call me? Skipsey, after the place I was born. I wouldn't get born there now, my mother wouldn't be allowed to stop long enough to have borned me. I wouldn't get born these days, me. Not like some," he added, looking at the baby. "And how's a little chuckler, then?"

Little chuckler bubbled.

Lall could think about Lavender's name, Skipsey, of course, but would not think she knew him well enough to use it. She wondered whether she would ever know the baby well enough to call it Rise. She was about to argue with Lavender about where you could be born, because Rise was not even a camping place; but Lavender was looking down the road towards the leaders of the coffle.

Laban Gozzle was down there, his secretive, soldiery bike still and silent, his feet on the ground. He was arguing. Then he kicked himself away, came up the pavement on the motor bike, and stopped by the engine.

"That gate across our ground," he said, and his bike thudded between words.

' You want me to take the engine down in front and

knock it flat?" said Lavender. "Do it in a minute, ready willing, and able, steam up and a big fire."

"Not first, not now, we've got to go in and ask about it first," said Laban. "But we can't get to do that, because, first, they want us to keep moving, the law says, keep moving. There's one of them down there now filling in our numbers. So we can't get out to ask, and they won't let us stop, not in any way."

"What do you reckon, then?" said Lavender. "Doing that to us."

"Not the law's fault," said Laban. "Thought it could be like this when I came yesterday. Look, I'll fix it for a minute. I can't do it to this one, Skipsey, you've got iron wheels, but I'll do it to your van, let the air out of a tyre; we can't shift then – right up the line we've got soft tyres, as soon as I've been along. It will make a time for us; time to talk to someone. This is our place, our winter quarters. They can't give us No Entry on that. We've got to make time; we've got to be so we can't move."

"Our problem is, we can't make time," said Lavender, "and our worry is, we aren't God people, we don't get time given." He jumped down from the engine and turned a tap along its side. Steam lifted into the air, hot, aromatic, oily, sighing and spluttering as it came out. "It won't work," said Lavender.

"What shall we do?" said Lall.

"I don't know," said Lavender. "Every man for himself. We've got no leader now, no chief like in the old days. We aren't people any more, not to houseys, not to ourselves. All right when I was born, but what did you come into the world for, little chuckler? No place for you here, right on from now."

"Beverley likes it," said Lall. "Selmah." Selmah, Beverley, were her sister's names. Lavender Skipsey would call her by her common name, Selmah, not Beverley.

"That's not enough," said Lavender. "He'll get to be a housey; he won't have us, he won't abide us. He'll not travel, he'll not pad the world, so what will he know? But what can change for us? No resting places now, no camps, no gaffs. It's bolt and bar and band on all the old gateways."

II

An Overnight

Issy Skirlaugh woke up unsettled on the morning the coffle was due to come down to its place between the mere and the sea. It would come, he knew; but would it, could it, stay?

He was already in that place, a housey person, which should have made him feel settled first of all. Perhaps you have to feel settled before you know about unsettled: today he felt quite clearly what it would be like to wander the roads for a whole lifetime.

Being unsettled made him get up early, but his mother was up earlier. Her name was Denah, Friday. He called her Friday, after the name of the place where she was born. She had come from the coffle years before, unsuited by an accident for the travelling life, and married here, and settled in a little black wooden house at the edge of the town, between the two waters of mere and sea, where the cold wind blows from one to the other.

She should have called him Skirlaugh, but since he was a housey, and had only housey friends, and went to school every term and every day, he was always called Issy. Friday said that if you mixed with people you got the proper way of doing things broken up and spoilt. Issy was short for Issachar, a good coffle name.

Friday was supping tea. She had a pot by the fire all the time. She sat by the fire with the door open and the first light of the day coming in with the wind. She kept the house like a living-van, the walls panelled and the floor suitably unsteady.

She shook her head slowly and hunched back in the cushions of her couch, adjusting them to suit her bad leg. The floor moved, like the floor of a van.

"You wait, Issy Skirlaugh," she said. "There'll be staves out; there'll be truncheons, there'll be things heavier than wooden spoons. Full of blood, you mark it, full of blood."

Issy felt more unsettled. He felt excited too, with Friday promising a battle before the day was over.

"When the coffle comes," she said, "we'll see a broken head or two."

When the coffle came each year, Issy saw a great deal of it, because the fields where it lodged were just down the lane that went past the house. Each year, when it came, he wondered where it had come from (he had misty visions of Moscow and Madagascar, North Pole, New York); and wondering visions of where it was going when it went after the winter (and longings to go to Azerbaijan or Australia, Patagonia or Plymouth).

Today, for the first time, he felt something of what it would be like to be taking your house wherever you went, the house staying the same, the world moving round you day by day.

It wasn't that he wanted to go, but suddenly he understood how life could be lived like that. And he understood too what it would be like to bring your house, your village of people, to a place that was the enemy.

"Maybe it's our heads will get broken," said Friday.

"We're not-on both sides; enemies twice if we ain't clear and careful."

Issy thought about that. When he came from school the day before he had seen the workmen of Burton Farms putting barbed wire along the side of the lane, where it came to the gate. He had gone down and watched a padlock being fastened to the gate with great bolts, and seen the notice screwed to the bars: KEEP OUT. PRIVATE. Burton Farms Ltd. E. Barker.

One of the men putting the notice, the bolts, the wire, in their places had been Robert Dent, his own father. His father had nodded him to go back home.

He had come back himself at the end of his day.

"I'm bound to do the work he gives me," he said, "or I'll lose my job."

Friday had gone out to look at the work. Her bad leg always seemed to go with her unwillingly. She limped down to the gate, looked at the wire, at the bolt, fingered the padlock, touched the notice, and came back.

"Keep out, is that it?" she said. She had missed reading when she was young. ("What of it?" she said. "I can't fly neither, so I shan't break no more bones that way.")

"We'd better stop out of it," said Issy.

"We don't want to do that," said Friday. "I don't mind getting my head broke. Look, I've got a bad leg, and hirple about; I get a bad head, maybe I'll think one side quicker than the other, that's all. No harm comes to me, Skirlaugh."

"Still," said Issy, "Dad's job. He likes to do that."

"That's real housey talk," said Friday. "But it's right, for all that it's housey words. We can't lose him his work. I came off the coffle and married him proper, not like they do on the road, but with a vicar minister, and I've to stand by all he stands for."

"Then what can we do?" said Issy. "That gate locked up, that notice, they're to keep the coffle out." And he thought of it turning away again, for Manchester or Manitoba, Abyssinia or Aberystwyth.

"I sat here tonight and drunk quarter of a pound of tea, I'd say," said Friday. "How about that for thinking? Well, naturally I thought of something, and a bit sooner than I need, dealing with all the houseys that never rise the same day they get up but tomorrow." She meant that house people rose late in the day.

"What'll you do?" said Issy. He was used to his mother's name, and accustomed to her way of thinking and speaking—a roundabout way, in fact, quite natural for a girl from the coffle.

"While I've been sitting in here, there's my old girls outside been laying me eggs," said Friday.

"You don't want to be throwing good eggs at Barker," said Issy. "Haven't you some bad ones?"

"You think of nothing," said Friday, "you housey. No, but a box or two of them, well, they don't get resisted, they don't get turned away, not if they get given, a box of eggs, a box of fresh eggs, you can't say no. And then when you've got them, what do you do?"

"I don't know I like eggs," said Issy. "Not above all."

"But if you've got them, took them in your hand; accepted them, belonged them; well, you get to give something in return, if I don't want payment for them, if I don't want anything for them."

"But you do want something for them," said Issy. "You don't understand what you're doing, and I don't know what you're talking about."

"I do," said Friday. "Take a sup of tea, boy, and you'll understand it too. No, look and listen. There you've got the eggs, free gift. Then, you see, I just want this little favour from you, and what are you going to do?"

"I'm going to give you your favour," said Issy. "I can tell. But what favour? And who am I?"

"That's it," said Friday. "I'm going to get my favour. I thought it up in the night, by the fire here. But I tell you what, I promise you I could do it without the eggs, just off my word of mouth, and it's safer too, because you could give back the eggs and say no, but if you don't get nothing to give back, you can't. But you'll see who you are when we get there. Rake up the fire, Issy, and I'll wake Dent and set him on his way to breakfast."

And with that she got up out of her chair, put her hand on the worn place on the dresser, where she always held and pushed to get herself going, and went across the room to the door of the stairs, and took her way up, leaning over in the narrow space. She went up like a grub in a grub run, she said.

Issy raked up the fire and sent the flames under the oven. A separated coil of smoke lifted from the grate and cycloned across the room, smelling tarry.

He closed the door. Traffic was beginning to go by in the road at the head of the lane, headlamps looking in at him as he laid bacon in the frying pan.

Then he wanted to open it again and see whether the outdoors had changed as much as his indoor self wanted it to. He wanted more than the house would give him. He wanted to see the coffle, to be the coffle, to feel the night that surrounded it, to taste the rising day that lighted it, to join its faraway places, its distant travels. He wanted to loosen from the things that bound his hands (at the moment sticky rashers of bacon) and be free in the moving world...Archangel, Samarkand, Skirlaugh itself...places that flavoured the coffle.

Bacon cooking, bread warm by the fire, stilled his feet. He was almost fixed again by the time the meal was over. And he could see how he mixed everything up, the wandering of the coffle and the thing it was actually wanting to do, settle down for the winter in one place, the fields where NO ENTRY was large on the gate.

His father went to work. "Don't loss me my job," he said. "Orders, mind, Denah." He had never become used to the way her name worked the other way round from most people's. He could not understand Friday. "Don't get calling me Cottage Memorial Hospital," he said, "which is where I was born."

Friday would remind him that she had been born under a hedge, and all the better for the touch of green grass round her bottom when she first sat down.

Issy had been born in the house, one day when his mother happened to be home, she told him. He thought for a long time that he would never have been found if she had been out at the time, and come back not knowing he had arrived.

"Now we'll set out," said Friday. "We'll go to Barker's cousin. Don't you ever think of things? He can't get the sack of anyone, because he's out of work. He wouldn't say no to a nice egg, but I'm not going to offer him one. But he can give us what we want for the coffle, can Colin Mr Morton; and then get the eggs."

"Mr Colin Morton," said Issy. "He comes to school sometimes and takes a lesson. Language."

"We all got language," said Friday. "No wonder he don't get much work. But he has a thing we need, and I'll get it off him. I've just got to forget him how he is with his cousin."

Forgetting him how he was with his cousin took Friday about half an hour. "We got to get there first," she said. "Me gambolling along like I do."

They went along a lane leading beside the mere. The lane turned into a track across the meadows. Long shadows set up by the early sun lay across the mere. The water lay still and smoking, darted by birds, seamed with ripples from risen fish, hemmed by trees, embroidered with its two islands, Swan and Temple.

Colin Morton lived at Temple Farm, no longer used for farming, in the village of Goose Hill.

"Gozzle," said Friday, saying Goose Hill as it was pronounced.

Colin Morton was up. "Doing nothing, just going for a swim. Dent," he said, "Mrs Dent."

"Denah's my common name," said Friday. "Do you want us to come in?"

"Not really," said Colin Morton.

"I call that polite," said Friday. "Straight and honest."

"House is untidy," said Colin. "You can come in and put up with it." He was a squarish tidy-looking man himself, but his house was not tidy. But it was not dirty. Friday went in and sat herself by the fire.

"I got to sit," she said. "Or else keep walking. Now I'll be straight out with a thought, polite like. I know Barker has the meadows and all the rest out to the sea, but we got right on some of it, and he oughtn't to stop us but he did, wiring up the gate and all. But the coffle, that's my folk in their vans and all their stuff, they're coming today, like always. So what if they set down in that back paddock of yours that's empty now?"

Colin thought about that. Friday repeated it to herself to see it had been right, since it had come out so fast.

"An overnight will do," said Friday. "While they see about Barker. And we thought to bring you some eggs, to pay you a present for listening."

"I don't need that," said Colin. "I've thought about it anyway. I don't care about cousin Edwin Barker, but I'm kin to him, so I'll charge the coffle for the overnight on my land. The difference is, I need the money, and Edwin doesn't."

"Well then," said Friday, "I was wrong about you."

"You might be," said Colin. "I don't care what anyone thinks."

"Nor do I," said Friday. "I thought I'd be half an hour drawing you round, but I did it in two minutes. All settled."

"Settled," said Colin. "When they come I'll tell them where to go. Now I'm off for a morning swim round the island and back."

Issy helped Friday up. They left. Issy put the eggs on the table—they stayed.

Out on the mere, as they went, nothing had changed, but as they walked along the shore first a shower of rain over the water turned the cloth of the surface wrong side up; then Colin plunged in and ripped the fabric open.

"I hear they got a baby in the coffle," said Friday. "I want to see that. There's no plenty of babies these days; just the two since your day. Now we'll go home and await. We'll await."

Colin splashed in the water as he swam, gently, like a tangle of cotton threads.

III

The Knot

Laban was Lall's father, as well as leader of the coffle. So when a limping woman came up the road and asked for Laban, Lall said, "Gozzle? He's up the line fixing things."

"I've gone further than I'm going," said the limping woman, and leaned on the engine wheel to rest her leg. Lall knew who she was, Denah Friday, who used to be a coffle girl but was now a housey. Lall thought she seemed to have more importance than a housey ought to have.

"Did that baby get born?" asked Friday, in her most complicated way: all babies are somehow born.

"My sister's," said Lall. She knew what Friday meant.

"I heard there was one," said Friday. "I near run my leg off coming up here. Wait until I get my breath back; and where's that Laban?"

Laban could be heard up the line, or his bike could, snapping and snarling at people. The road, because it was blocked, had no moving traffic on it, and people had begun to flow on to it, and had to be snarled at.

Selmah Beverley began to walk up the line from a front wagon. Lall thought she would be glad to hand the baby over. But when Friday asked to hold it she said "No" at once, and moved away.

"I've got to have it sometime," said Friday.

"Not now," said Lall. "It's ours."

"It's mine," said Selmah, arriving and taking the baby.

"Well, no matter," said Friday. "I'll have him later."

"You shan't," said Selmah.

"We'll see," said Friday.

"Now, girls," said Lavender, "now Selmah Beverley, Denah Friday, and Lall Routh. And baby."

"Now Lavender Skipsey," said Denah. "And do you see that boy of mine?"

"Issachar Skirlaugh?" said Lavender. "Down in the distance, idling by a wagon. What are they doing? Pumping up a tyre? They don't want to be doing that. We've got nowhere to go, so we're stopping here."

"You've got friends," said Friday. "Houseys think of you, if you don't think of houseys. And this housey fixed you up a night, and I daresay you can spin it out a night or two more."

Laban Gozzle came down the line. "Now then, Denah," he said. "It's a short visit. We've got to see somebody. We have to get something fixed."

Selmah said, "Come on, Lall, we'll fix up the baby," and she and Lall left the steam engine and the sorting out of what was to happen next. "Who's Big-eyes Beauty Smellifer by name?" said Selmah. "Who's Gladwrap Gorgeous Galloper, eh?"

They took it into the trailer where they lived. Their mother was in already, setting a fire in the stove, and a kettle to boil. Their mother's name was Jane Ellerby. They called her Ellerby; most other people called her Jane.

"What does Denah Friday want, coming along so

soon?" said Jane. "She's generally a bit shyer than that."

"Got a place for the vans to set down," said Lall. "She was saying."

"It's called a knot," said Jane. "Don't forget words and ways."

"She got a place for the knot, then," said Lall.

"Shut the door then," said Jane. "We shouldn't be in here when we're travelling."

Selmah began to undo the baby, to change it. "Peter Pittle Pottle," she said, making up more rude names for it as she did so.

"Gozzle got anything to say about it?" asked Jane.

"He hadn't heard when we came off," said Selmah. "There now, Booby Belly Billy, what a lovely tummy, and what's this, eh? He's got a lovely clear tummy, Ellerby, but turn him on his face, and he's got these freckles on his back, there, at his shoulders, and across his belt, and on his little bum."

"Birth marks," said Jane. "They won't mortify, you needn't think it. But we'll see what it means. You don't get things like that meaning nothing. Denah Friday knows more than most; she's been sat there remembering, not going about picking up new and forgetting the old. You'll have to give it over to her later, if we get settled in a knot."

The baby got his dry clothes, and something to eat. The engine, now further away from Lall, hooted twice, Laban Gozzle drove past, and the trailer moved forward a few feet, then stopped. Gozzle came back up the line, with more instructions. He explained later that the front of the coffle, being stuck in the lane leading to a blocked gate, had had to come out, take a trip round the town, and find its way into a lane it had already passed. In time the trailer moved again, down the road, turning into a lane, then bumping along a track by the water of the mere, so coming to Goose Hill, to a place near the proper site but not it at all.

When the coffle stopped, and the knot was being formed, the proper way the vans were arranged, Lall came out to see what an argument was going on about.

"Don't take notice, Colin Mr Morton," Friday was saying. "Don't listen. I tell you, Laban Gozzle, you might be on home ground where you got born, right over there in those fields, but this time, this winter, you've got lucky to be here at all."

"But Friday," said Laban, "we must have water running. We don't drink standing water, we don't drink the mere. That's for the horses, and engines."

"You haven't got no horses," said Friday. "And if you don't want to stop here, well, undo the knot, take the coffle away. Colin Mr Morton, that's educated and writing books, he just lent you this field out of his own kindness of mind, and he doesn't know what you think about standing water."

"I tell you what, Mrs Dent," said Colin Morton, who was quite interested but not upset by what was going on, "I don't care what he thinks about standing water. If it isn't good enough he can go; but if he's going then let him go at once. Otherwise there's a tap back in the yard at the house, and he can draw from that. He doesn't have to say thank you. But if he stays I want ten pounds each day at noon."

A Land Rover came down from the town, across the meadows to the knot. In it was E. Barker, of Burton Farms Limited, with his moustache that tended to be greenish with tobacco smoke.

"Now, Colin," he said, "what's this?"

"I'm off," said Friday. "I don't want him coming back

on Dent out of my fault." She limped away. "Send on that Issy," she said. "Barker might know him."

Issy, understanding that things might be awkward for his father, had already slipped away, although he wanted to know what was to happen.

"It's good to see you, Edwin," said Colin. It was a bone-hard lie.

"What are all these gypsies doing here?" said Edwin Barker. "You can't have them here. They've no right here, any more than they have a right in my fields. I've gone into it, and they haven't."

Laban Gozzle was about to tell him something, probably of a disagreeable kind, more threats than meaning. But Jane Ellerby stepped clatterpan out of her trailer kitchen, and stood like a snake.

"Gypsy?" she said. "Who is calling me a gypsy? Who is giving me the wrong sort of name? What ignorant person?"

"We aren't talking names, Ellerby," said Laban, mildly. "Just about rights and such." He thought that since he was not calling Edwin Barker all sorts of names (like "Peter Pittle Pottle", perhaps, Lall thought), the names did not for the moment matter.

"Who said gypsy?" said Jane Ellerby, taking no notice of Laban Gozzle. She stood on the step of the trailer, speaking very hard and clear, being exact. Of course, she was called gypsy every day of the summer, and did not mind. Now she was picking a quarrel with the enemy.

E. Barker looked at her and said nothing. Lavender and some other men came round behind him. Issy, looking back, saw him being surrounded, and watched, but nothing came of it.

"Gypsy, eh?" said Jane, fixing Edwin Barker with her eye.

"Travellers," said Edwin Barker. "Travellers."

"There," said Jane. "Nothing wrong with gypsies, mind, but things have to be right."

"And they are right," said Edwin Barker. "You people can't come on my land, and you can't do anything about it, because I've made certain, and everybody here knows it. And you can't stop here either, not beyond a night."

"Four nights," said Colin. "I've looked into it too. But they're welcome to that. And if I could make it more I would."

"But I came to say, Keep Out," said Edwin Barker. "Keep out of my land; keep out of my lake, keep out of my woods, keep off the islands. I mean to get you driven out."

"Very fairly spoken," said Jane.

"Right enough," said Laban. "But what you don't know about you can't prove, mister, so watch out for things you don't know who did them."

"Fairly spoken too," said Colin. "And you haven't any right on here, Edwin, so I'll understand if you go."

"I'll be watching," said Edwin. "Gypsies or no."

Lavender and the other men stood away and let him go to his Land Rover.

As he went Lavender gave him a blast on the whistle of the engine. Issy, hearing the blast, looked round and saw all was calm. A moment later the Land Rover swung past him, throwing mud out of the track over the meadow.

At the coffle it was time to eat and rest. After that Lavender, Laban, and others went round the outside of the knot with wires. They were not putting up a fence, though Laban could remember being told of times when a coffle or a knot had to have defences. They were linking up the electrical system, and as the day grew darker Lavender brought pressure up on the engine and set it to drive a generator, so that lights could go on, and television sets work. It is marvellously cosy in a well-run knot.

Before dark had come down Jane and other women had gathered wood. Edwin Barker, if he had been watching them, would not have known where they got it, but it must have come from his woodland. It was for a fire in the middle of the knot.

When it was well going and the flames and the reflections of the flames stood in the shining sides and windows of the vans in the circle, the television sets went off and the people came out dressed neatly, to stand by the fire, waiting. This was not only the first night in the winter quarters, the winter knot, but the night the baby was shown and named.

Into the circle limped Denah Friday and Issachar. She came here now because she had special knowledge and memories and experiences; more than Jane Ellerby had; and she had a particular place among the people, though she was a housey.

"It's bad," she said, when she had settled. "If you've got just a cushion under that side, my dear, or I won't be able to hop and go after. There, ta. He's got the whole place set against you, except I got my good Colin Mr Morton, he's a good sort and done it for you. But he took your rights and dealt them to death, and I hear that's the law of it. You can't get in on his land."

"We got to come under the law," said Laban. "Obey it. So what do we do? Move on? Do they want to run us out of the country?"

Yes, thought Lall. Away for ever.

Hyderabad, Hobart, thought Issy. I would go.

"We'll have to come to think of that," said Friday. "But first let's see about that baby, what I come down for now; let's look at it by the firelight."

That was, just now, more important than the future. It was time for the baby to be shown, now that the knot for the winter had been made, and even if it could not endure.

The people came closer. The flames grew higher, and the smoke swirled. For now there was only this place, lit, sheltered, safe, no matter what the rest of the world was like, or whose it all was outside.

"Maybe the last time for any of this," said Lavender.

"We'll look at it," said Friday. "Yes, we'll see what sort it is, man or woman, and we'll get it some names. You got the names, Beverley?"

"Yes," said Selmah.

"And the baby?" said Friday. "Let's have the baby first then. My, you got it tied up tight. I hope you got a steel pin somewhere about, to keep off bad things. Yes. Now, out he comes; there, has Friday a cold finger then. Now, first thing, man or woman. I declare, proper little man." That was a well-known secret already; no one heard anything fresh. "But what's this, Beverley? What's this on his back? Was he born with these markings? Was he born so?"

"Yes," said Selmah. "Do you want his names now?"

"They won't mortify," said Jane. "Will they?"

"No," said Friday. "They won't mortify, and no, we can't have names. I do believe you can't have names. There's a big difficulty," she said slowly. "Help me up. I have to say this standing."

She was helped up by Lall and Issy. She leaned on Issy and gave Lall the baby to hold, naked and warm, very unwrapped, firelight in his eyes, walking on Lall's chest.

"Hold him up," said Friday. "They all have to see; and he has to see who he's with."

How public, thought Lall. How very showing. I hope they didn't do this to me.

In a moment it was clear they never did that to her. Friday went on speaking. "You all see the markings on him – hold him up, child – see the starmarks right across his back, on shoulder and belt and buttock, the mark of the wheel. This is something rare, this is. This is something different from a regular baby. I believe, and take my word for it, I believe this is a chief, and we got to find the old chief at once and get the right names. This is our chief, I believe, and he'll have to be named in a bigger fashion than we can do it now. We'll need a knot and a half to name him."

Friday stopped speaking, and looked round at a silent audience. It was a dignified and solemn moment. The baby marked the occasion by leaving a large damp memorial on Lall's dress front.

"Pittler," she said, and all the dignity went.

"Chief Pittler," said Selmah Beverley. "I always said he was a special little stinker."

IV

A Fair Exchange

Selmah wrapped up the special little stinker again. "Have you waved him around enough, then?" she asked first.

"We saw what we had to see," said Friday.

"You couldn't have seen more," said Selmah. "Have I to do anything different, now he's a chief? Is his own mother's milk good enough for him yet?"

"Nobody will take him away from you," said Friday. "But it was different in the old days, I recall, when there was plenty of families, and the chief had the best from all. But there was never a baby like that in my time, never. I just know what my mother and grandmother might have said."

Selmah was packing the baby into his wrappings, tight and trim. "Where's the iron pin?" she said. "And there's its father to have his say about him when he lands home again. It isn't like the old days, Denah."

"No," said Friday, "there's a lot changed. But something has come back; something has returned to us, because that's a certain sure chief. And," she added, "I'm shocked you didn't know, Ellerby."

Jane looked at her and shook her head. "We have

had to forget," she said and others nodded, to show they meant the same thing—as if they meant to forget.

Lall was lowering Friday down to her cushions again, not knowing how best to hold. Issy, the other side of her, was doing the the same thing but not watching. He was noticing how the gathering of people round the fire had begun to break up, without speaking, and go in ones and twos to the trailers, close the doors, and switch on lights.

They don't want to know, thought Lall. They've switched on the lights and switched off the thing about the chief.

Issy, letting his mother manage for the last few inches to the ground, looked back at what had been there a minute or two earlier, when the people had stood in a listening silence, when the importance of Friday's words, the intense flavour of the instant had come upon them all. Then it had all gone; the people had turned away and forgotten as soon as they could.

"Help me up again," said Friday. "I've said it, I've said it, but it's like it was unbegun of and they haven't heard. Now, Ellerby (just put your arm under mine, Lall dear, that's it), Jane Ellerby, you have to make sense into these people, and I'll be back tomorrow."

"Ah," said Jane Ellerby, "but there's something, isn't there, Denah Friday?"

"I'll come tomorrow," said Friday. "But where's the Bird Man? The Bird Man and his Menagerie?"

"The Bird Man is wintering the other side," said Jane. "In Ripon, along with Doubtfire."

"Then, Issy, we'll tramp off. But remember, Jane, remember you all, you've got a chief, and you want that; it's what you haven't got that you don't want, and we have to find out about that."

Friday left the firelight, left the knot, left the coffle, and she and Issy faded into the meadow.

"What is it?" said Lall. "What did they remember? Why did they all go away? What's wrong with the baby?"

"Nothing," said Jane. "Nothing. They remembered something we all have to forget; something they didn't even do, but it's on us whether we want or not."

Now that Friday had gone trailer doors opened, and people began to come out and stand or sit by the fire again. Laban Gozzle went into one of the lorries and brought out the long bar and the posts that held it, to put across the fire. He brought the large kettle, unused since the last knot, and Lavender went across the fields to fill it at the tap. Laban put the bar across the fire, hung a chain on it, and then hung the kettle on the chain.

"Some of us joined in what we did together," said Laban when he had looked round to see that everyone was there. "We're all part of it. But I don't know, the world changed so in my time, you get a young man like Lavender, you've never heard of a chief, have you?"

"I heard there used to be one," said Lavender. "But we've got used to the little man with the big mouth acting boss, and that was plenty."

Laban laughed at that. "There's sparrows, and there's cock sparrows," he said. "But there was a chief once. And the thing is, now he's dead."

"He's dead," said Jane Ellerby. "I heard, dead."

"Dead, no other word," said Nazar Wawne. "If we've got a new chief, that's good enough for me, and Fahkri would be plenty pleased."

Fahkri was Selmah's man, the baby's father. He was away now, a missionary in Doncaster.

"We can forget about the old times," said someone else. "Why should we carry that? We weren't there."

"I was," said Nazar. " I remember. I was four years old. Friday is my sister. I say forget what she has to say, and have the little man as chief."

"He means the baby, not Gozzle," said Lavender.

"Kettle's boiling," said Jane. So instead of talking about the chief any longer, they had tea, and the fire stopped flaming and fell into red embers, and then began to coat with ash. The kettle, hung at the edge now, swung a little and the remaining water hissed against its side.

Lall's face burned cold when she got up. The night burned dark into her eyes as well. Lavender went to the engine and damped it down for the night. The electric lamps began to glow less bright.

"What is it all, what are we talking about?" asked Lall, as she got to bed next to the baby.

"I don't get to tell you, even if I knew," said Jane Ellerby. "Something they did, we did, to the last chief."

"Less talk of that," said Gozzle.

"And this one's my baby," said Selmah. "I'll say for him."

Down town, Friday was in a telephone box. "Just leave me," she said to Issy. "I can't fall out."

But she had to call Issy in, because her reading was too slow and inaccurate for her to make out the instructions. She had a primitive way of managing, in which she picked up the handset and spoke into it, hoping to get a reply without dialling. But all the telephone would do nowadays was buzz at her.

"You've seen it on television, Fride," said Issy.

"They never rung up anyone I knew," said Friday. "Go on then, get me to Doubtfire at Ripon. Him I know, and he'll get me to the Bird Man, which that isn't his name."

So Issy went through directory enquiry, and wrote the number down, and then searched the code book. He dialled, and got the Doubtfire number. The message was short. Friday took the phone and said, "Clark Riston, come to the coffle at Burton in the morning. We got Nine Bright Shiners. This is Denah Friday. And we're getting evicted."

"There," she said, pushing the door open and coming into the street again, "that's fixed that."

"I want to know what it's all about," said Issy. Ripon, he thought, Rome, Middlesborough, Mordor.

"Little place by the church," said Friday. "In my time we had a chief. Of course, you can't make anything of this, but I was his mother. They made me his mother. There's more to it than that, and I've forgotten it. I'd be three years old, no more. Running about then, I was, not hirpling like this. But there, accidents happen. Now we'll get home and see Dent."

Home, thought Issy. Arcturus, the Pleiades, the dusty hill of the Milky Way. Home is where you take it.

Lall, waking, thought, If he is a chief why can't he speak to E. Barker, showing his power, making the rights of the coffle clear?

"Why not, Gozzle?" she asked. "Why not, Ellerby?"

"Dafter things have worked," said Jane.

"And dafter things haven't," said Laban.

Lall thought it was a clear idea, and the only one she had, and that it should be tried. However, no one got up very soon at the knot, so there was no one to ask. The baby itself was still asleep.

Before anything happened in the knot, things began to happen outside it. A van came nosing its way across the meadows. For a place where no one was awake the knot became very observant, with eyes at every window. Lavender's dog went out and spoke to the van severely, stopping it in the track for a time. But it came on and came on, and lodged itself in a space among the vehicles.

On its side was written, "Clark Riston, Bird Man, Menagerie, Rare Species".

"She sent for him," said Laban Gozzle. He left the trailer and went to the new arrival. The door of it slid back, jumbling the writing, and out stepped another small man, like Laban. But he had a beard, and was wearing a strange garment like a cloak, that looked at first like glossy knitting, and then like something painted. But it turned out to be patterned with the small feathers of birds, laid and stitched, blue, red, gold, mottled brown, dense black, the sheeny iridescence that would turn water.

He had come towards the end of the night, knowing where the coffle should be, coming down the lane past Friday's house. She had sat waiting in the cabin of a room, her second night there drinking tea. She heard the van go down the lane and meet the barred gate, and come out backwards.

She had gone out and stopped Clark Riston, and brought him in brilliant within the four walls, and given him tea. Sleeping monkeys opened once and closed their eyes, wrapped in rugs in the back of the van. Issy came down and saw the great vestment and the man inside, drinking tea with lips, not a beak.

"Troubles they don't want to remember," Friday was saying, "troubles they should remember."

"I remember," said the Bird Man, "and I wish I could not. Ah, Friday, you have only heard; there is nothing you know about the time. But you should remember most, perhaps."

"I should," said Friday. "But accidents will happen."

"What we did was not an accident," said the Bird Man, and he raised a lustrous arm as he drank tea, and the colour from the arm, like the colour from a wing, flowed on to the wall and the ceiling, and Issy thought the beginnings of flight might be occurring, to tramp the tropic clouds like the flocks of Java, the migrant swallows, the congregate birds of paradise. Issy sat by the fire asleep.

Clark Riston had papers on which things were written. It was a thing not approved of by the people of the coffle. Lall thought of the paper as another sort of decoration on Clark Riston. Clark Riston wrote on the papers too, using the long feather of a bird, blue and brown like eyes, a quill; and a black ink in a traveller's bottle.

"More than eighty years since we had Nine Bright Shiners," he said. "More than eighty years since we had a chief born. So a good thing it's written down, the way we do it. If there's Nine Bright Shiners born, that's the chief. That's what it is, even if there's one already."

"We haven't one already," said Laban Gozzle.

"Ah," said Clark Riston.

"Ah," said Friday. "That we don't know and have to find. Because he has to be there, and hand over. I remember."

"And I remember, too," said Nazar Wawne. "I recall we left the chief senseless and starving in his van, dying, fifty or more years since. So he's dead."

"And we have nothing from him at all," said Nazar. "All except what Friday has."

"Accidents will happen," said Friday. "I was his

mother. You understand a chief has to have a mother all his life, so I was made his. I was three years old. He was a grown man, more than thirty. I think he got a little merry at one gaff, and took me in his arms and dropped me, out of the Wheel it was. I liked the ride up there. Dropped me, his own mother. So he gave what he had, compensation, blood money, all he had, except his van; horse and all he gave, and then we couldn't give back."

"We couldn't help," said Nazar. "What he gave he had to give. Just his van he had, in the snow, in a knot at Hollym, where we kept horses. No horses now. He paid up, and he was left to die."

"These things are written down," said Clark Riston. "These things are known; what was due, what could be given. But he never gave the chief's things; they stayed in his van. That's what we need, to tell your rights to have a knot, winter quarters; and there is something here to prove your rights belong here, if you can find that. But in the end only the chief knows; only the chief has knowledge. Only the old chief can tell how to make the new chief after him, what you have here."

"No good asking Stinker," said Selmah.

"I remember," Clark Riston went on, taking no notice. "I remember too. We left him, senseless he was, starving and without coals, in his van at the beginning of the snows, in that empty field. We heard of him no more. But I think he lived, even if he was left for dead. And we have to find him. And I say that boy should go forth and find him."

And he looked at Issy, sitting a quarter way round the fire from him. And he flung a feathered arm towards him. "Are you not his brother?"

"Where?" said Issy, with his mind running towards New York or Namibia, Kamchatcka or Carlisle.

"Try Hull," said Clark Riston.

"Oh," said Issy. He had been to Hull; it was not far enough; you get there by bus, the ride to nowhere. "I'll go," he said.

"Go and get us our rights," said Laban.

"Aye," said Denah Friday, his own mother, "get you gone."

"I'll take a dish of tea before I go," said Clark Riston, folding his papers, his business done.

V

New Homes

The monkeys in the back of the van were having talks of their own, discussing their food. When Issy climbed into the van again the meeting broke up and their large beautiful eyes, like some continuity and condensation of their fur, began to quiver uneasily, and the whites to show under the lids.

Clark Riston got in at the other side, stowing his papers under the seat, dropping the quill on the grass outside, to show that a wild foreign bird had flown that way.

"You don't want to be coming in with me," he said. "I'm off back to Doubtfire's. I have my trade to care for. I've dealt with your business."

Issy got out of the van. Clark Riston was right: his part of things was over. Issy had only got into the van while he thought what he was to do, what he was doing, thinking simply of riding home.

Clark Riston had said he should go, and what for and where; but no one else had taken much notice of that. When Clark Riston got up to go, without being thanked, without saying that he was leaving, the meeting had gone on. It was still going on. Issy slid the door of the van shut, and the monkeys whimpered. The van backed and turned and left. There was only the quill on the grass. Issy picked it up. The ink lay wet on its shaft. A drop of rain fell on the curve of the feather, ran down, and mingled with the ink. Black blood from a wounded eagle.

"I don't know what Dent would say," Friday was telling the coffle. "What's Clark Riston to him? he'll say, come and gone leaving nothing but a word that he's to send Issy out on the world."

"Just left a feather, Friday," said Issy. "And only Hull. That's not far. It's not far enough."

"It wasn't just his meaning," said Laban Gozzle.

"Hull for a starter," said Nazar Wawne. "There's not much at Hull, Friday. We never went to that fair in my time, and wouldn't be let a place if we did."

Issy's thoughts began to get clearer. When Clark Riston first spoke Issy had dreamed of grand distances; when he had spoken of Hull at the end of the bus ride Issy had felt something was taken away from him, which was why he had gone to the van, thinking that he might ride home in it if nothing was to happen here. But now Kalgoorlie, Karachi, Great Bear Lake, Mare Tranquillitatis, were on the map again.

Or perhaps they were more real than that. Laban Gozzle was speaking again. "Clark has it in his mind, and on his papers," he said. "He knows who's who."

"I reckon he knows where Shemer Burlington is," said Nazar Wawne.

"Shemer Burlington," said Laban Gozzle. "That's the chief."

"Yes," said Friday. "I didn't want to be the first with his name. Shemer Burlington."

"Somebody has to look," said Laban. "Somebody has to come with us, because we've got to go, no doubt about that. Somebody has to find Shemer Burlington and tell him he isn't chief any more, and then he's bound to tell what he knows about our place here, our winter quarters. And who's got to go is Issy, it isn't any of us already, but a fresh one. Riston knows."

"Well then, I still have to deal with Dent," said Friday. "He won't want just me about the van, about the house. I tell you what, you give me this girl here, while you have my boy, and then I'll have a help, and maybe Dent won't notice too hard."

It was Lall she was looking at.

"I'd like to be a housey for a bit," said Lall. "Eh?"

"Evens it up all round," said Friday.

"Give and take," said Laban. "And Clark Riston says we have to search here too—she can do that: she can find the thing that's here already."

"That she can," said Nazar. "She can look in on this Mister Farmer and seek out the hooks and hangers of it all."

"Issy could do that," said Lall, letting herself waver a little. "What is it? What are they?"

"He won't be here," said Laban. "And he don't know."

"It all suits me," said Lall, rallying again, seeing hearth and home, out of the wind's way. "I'd like it."

"It all suits me," said Issy. Kilkenny, Krakatoa, Crusaderville, came to his mind.

"Is it right with you, Ellerby?" said Laban. He was not fond of asking Jane's opinion, but since it was obvious that Issy would take Lall's place, bed, table and all, she had to be consulted.

"Right by me," said Jane. "He'd best call me Ellerby, in the family like. But one thing we have to do for you before we begin, Issy Skirlaugh (Skirlaugh I'll call you), and that's get you looking right: you look like a real housey housey." She was ready for what she had to do.

She sat Issy down on the steps of the van, tipped his head up, left ear on top, applied something to the lobe of the ear, and squeezed.

Issy's face felt it, and writhed before the rest of him. Then he found a drop of blood on the ear (he thought it might be black like the ink on the feather) and a gold ear-ring wired to the nerves, filling a space in him that was not there. A silver tear-drop stood in his eye on that side.

"One of us now," said Jane.

Issy touched the ring cautiously, wondering why it had to be put in red hot; but that was his ear being angry.

"Best done quick," said Jane. "Now all is changed and done, what do we do, Gozzle?"

"We pack up and go," said Laban. "Ten pound to the man, and off we go before noon."

"I'll get steam up," said Lavender.

Friday and Issy went home. "It stands to reason you take your own clothes," said Friday. "But everything else is the same for boy and girl. Ten to one Dent won't notice, or if he does he says nothing, you watch; but he won't complaint about it. He doesn't complaint."

"I shan't be here to see," said Issy; but "You'll see," said Friday.

And Jane was saying to Lall, "Friday's no real housey, so you won't get wrong from her. It'll be right there; and you keep looking for what you can get, you don't just get left in fun. No, Friday can't get about, and it was no life for her, laid in a van, and he's a good man, Dent, and there's nothing wrong with outside people, even houseys sometimes. Beverley's Fahkri is a good boy, and he lived in a house in his country; and my own mother, Wawne's mother too, came out of the land, years back, to be with your grandad Roos. Here we are," she went on, thumping a dress into a plastic bag, "here we are, travelling people, and not a case or trunk to travel with. We live in the boxes with the goods."

"It'll be a change, in a house," said Lall.

"You want it?" said Jane.

"Friday isn't a housey," said Lall. "It'll be grand."

The knot began to break up. It was an operation more complicated than making the knot.

In the making all the sections came joined together, lorry with van, steam engine with trailer, and so on. All that has to be arranged is done by backing the vans into the circle, then unhitching.

Hitching up is more delicate, and takes time. Ground that is happy to take wheels already moving has a fashion of turning wet and slippery when a loaded lorry with a trailer wants to move away. Lavender had to be ready with a puff of steam now and then; or the spare truck had to push. Sometimes, as a last resort, the steam engine had to go out on to the hard road and pull with a wire rope and a winch. But that was not necessary today.

Colin Morton came down to see how things were.

"You'd be right for another three nights," he said. "And I could drop the rent a bit."

"It's not the rent," Laban said, driving a cotter into a tow-pin. "But the fact is, if we don't get a long stop for winter we can't find work locally, so we can't pay rent anyway. No, we've got reasons for going, like our own reasons, tribal, you might say."

"Are you a tribe?" said Colin. "What sort of tribe? Are you gypsies, or what?"

"I don't mind answering," said Laban. "But we have to go now. When we find out our rights we'll get back and then you come of a night and ask us. But just now we have to get on the way, or we shan't find a place for tonight, or we shan't reach it by dark."

Colin Morton nodded his head and went away. He was on his way to his morning swim.

"Frogged off," said Lavender, from the cockpit of the engine when Laban came up to speak to him about the next van. "Frogged off into the lake, I'm just waiting for a heron to get him," and he watched a little longer the plashy track of Colin's overarm strokes.

The knot unwound. The coffle began to assemble on the track over the meadows. Lall saw her van move without her, pulled up from its resting place, away from the remains of the fire, in line, and going away from her gradually.

She stood by the fire, and heard raindrops fall into its hot ashes and dry sharply.

No one said goodbye to her. They did not know much about goodbye in the coffle, and all of them were busy.

Colin Morton came out of the mere and strode off to his house to do whatever he did in the morning. He looked at the coffle, and at Lall, but he did not know they were separate.

Issy came running up the road far across the meadows. He wanted to ride on the engine, but he was taken up in the lorry where the ride was, to sit under the duck.

He does not know how to look after a baby, thought Lall. She kept having the thought, without knowing how to work it out. It had nothing much to do with Issy, in fact. It had more to do with how Lall felt about not having the baby to turn to and look after. The thought kept bothering her. She could not tell that she was missing the baby, and all the coffle and the people in it.

She kicked unburnt wood into the fire and made smoke and flame. It did not occur to her that she was homesick, because how can you be homesick for something that moves away from you, that moves anyway, that is not quite a place?

It all moved further away. It moved out of sight. It had not moved out of hearing, because now and then, for some long time, Lall heard the cheerful toot of the engine.

She spent that long time by the fire, looking at it, looking at the sudden empty place where the knot had been, at the flat land running to the mere where the little ripples lapped the shore; at the hedge with the coffle's own true fields beyond, and the sea further away out of sight. There was only herself and the wind from that cold sea, and the empty place. The emptiness filled a place that was not there.

After much of the long time had passed, Colin Morton came to look at her, seeing her standing alone with her hands open on her cheeks, thinking she might be lost and in any sort of trouble.

When he came she could not speak, because nothing could stop her being alone. She bowed her head and tears fell in the ashes, hissing away in steam.

Colin Morton went to Friday's house, and was sent to find Robert Dent, because Friday had walked all she could in the past days.

Robert Dent, not knowing what was about, left his work and came to Lall, and led her away, offering as he did to take the farm Land Rover and drive her to the coffle; but she shook her head and said No. The coffle set her to stay, and she would. So he brought her to his house and gave her over to Friday, knowing he would hear of it when his work was done.

VI

Through a Glass, Darkly

The tent grew in the dark wood like a great illuminated flower with a bell, harebell or bluebell, but parchment-coloured. Issy could not believe his sight. He had a fever, he knew he had a fever and felt ill, and now he wondered whether his eyes could not read what they saw. This pale glow must be light alone, not a lit thing; perhaps the moon approached.

Issy walked with the men, and ached at his joints and in his head, stumbling on the black woodland floor. He wanted to lie down. He had wanted comfort all day, even when he had been well.

He had thought of riding in the trailer sitting in an easy chair watching the land pass; or, what he had first imagined but not hoped, of assisting in the driving of the steam engine.

Neither thing had happened. Instead he had sat in the back of a lorry, with his knees against the gilded stalk of some strange roundabout beast, deciding it might be a porpoise, with nothing else possible. He sat on a hard floor, alone and cold.

Burton walked away from him. The road south trod

by. Mappleton crept past to seaward, to landward, abaft.

There was no sea coast of Zimbabwe, no reef of Serendib or Strait of Magellan. He and the lorry, the lorry and the coffle, wandered the familiar fields of Holderness. He knew some of the trees. They went down no unfamiliar byways, stepped over no boundary to fresh woods, entered no new pasture.

Issy had been round here on his bicycle. Anyone not stupid, he began to think, would have come here on it today. But he let the thought dry, because he knew the bicycle had not lifted him out of the common road. He hoped the coffle would do that.

The coffle had a long stop on a grass verge, from about noon to two o'clock. They were now slightly beyond Issy's cycling range, but were in the same sort of world, the same sort of country. It had an unreal, not quite pleasing look about it, as if he did not want to see it.

Jane cooked meat against a fire. The smell of it hung on Issy as it cooked. When he came to eat he found he had already taken enough by breathing, and could swallow nothing.

"It's the ride," said Jane, and ate it herself.

Laban Gozzle now said that he would go ahead on the grey motor bike and be sure there was a place to lodge in that night. "There's choices," he said, "but there isn't always choosing, not for us any more."

He asked Issy whether he would like to travel with him, as a change from the lorry. Issy said yes at once, and then thought that he would rather sit by a hedge for now. His ear bothered him a little, a heated ache in the lobe, where the gold ring hung. He fingered it. A wave of unhappy feeling went down his throat.

"Turn it," said Jane. He was too cautious to do it, so Jane reached out a hand and turned it for him. There was a pain with the turning, when the ear was touched, but the moving of the ring through the lobe was a non-feeling: something happened but he did not know what it was.

Jane put her hand on his forehead. "A fevery bit," she said. "I hope he's not smittled with anything."

"I'll go without him," said Laban.

"Yes," said Issy.

"I'll go," said Selmah, and off she went, clinging and waving and beaming.

"And us to maintain the baby," said Jane. "That was Lall's do, was that."

It was not Issy's do. He looked at the baby and found it was not conversational, so there was nothing to be said to it or about it.

They travelled in the cab of Nazar Wawne's wagon, Jane with the baby by the door, Issy wedged against the engine cover, growing hot and cold. Outside the fields went by, regular and irregular, green or ploughed, brown or grass and the windscreen cut the stalks of the rain so the transparent sap ran down as water. In the back of the wagon the packed struts of the Wheel rattled as if they still spun the chairs above the villages.

Issy's face grew hot and his mind blurred like the windscreen, and nothing wiped half circles in it to clear the view.

Laban met them on the road, and led them where they were to go. It was a new coast to Issy, but he could not care. The flat coast they had come to, with its long mud banks, its fading approach lane, its smudged distant shore, was only a place within his fever. He sat on the step of the wagon and the ground shook under his feet, and as the engine died down a buzzing silence crept into his head and stayed there.

Jane gave the baby to Selmah and took Issy away.

She put him to bed in Lall's blankets on a shelf that was as large as he wanted the world to be. She gave him a cup of tea, which he sipped but had to leave.

He pulled the blankets over himself and laid his head down. He had then to turn with his face to the van wall, because his ear was too painful to lie on.

Darkness came on him. It was all he wanted. He knew that at any moment Friday would come dot-and-carry into his room and ease him by being his mother. Even if she did not know what was wrong and shook her head, she was still with him.

It was Lavender who came and looked at him.

"Are you a doctor?" said Issy.

"Nothing of that," said Lavender. "We don't have that." He looked at Issy by electric light.

The knot had been set up for the night, and outside the steam engine gently turned and made current. Beyond that a tide had come up the great river and washed the shore.

"We'll take you along the road, eh, Jane, should we? I think we should get Paul and Jamaica to look."

"I wouldn't fuss, but it's Friday's boy," said Jane.

She helped Issy to get up. He banged his head on the wood above the bunk. He did not feel like standing straight, but he walked to the door. "Thank you, Ellerby," he said.

"We'll have you back right," said Jane. "Now, where's Lall...Oh, she isn't here."

Issy and Lavender had gone in the small truck, out through the darkness of these waterside moors, where now and then Issy felt they would come to the mere again. But the mere was not mounted by waves like these, or the close smell of incoming sea or outrunning river. He saw, with swaying head, land and sea swim together.

The road went through groves of trees, along the sides of fields, into a trackless wood, and gave up.

"We'll wait," said Lavender, switching off the engine but leaving the lights on. He gave three long blasts on the horn.

They waited. The wood seemed underwater; sting-rays glided dark in the branches, whales jumped over the moon; prawns twitched in the moss, flatfish soled the paths.

There was something at the window beside Issy. He recoiled from it, knowing it was a shark with moist open jaws and rows of teeth for ever. The only light was that reflected from tree trunks and pine needles, and by it he saw something and nothing. But all the world had softened into other things now.

"That's Jamaica," said Lavender, and the door his side opened, "here's Paul."

"Man," said Jamaica, opening Issy's door, and being not a shark but just as hard to see in the darkness, possibly an octopus, to Issy's dizzy mind, but in fact a very black man indeed. "Skipsey, we're right glad to see you."

"Jamaica Kingston," said Lavender, "and Paul Paull. And this is Issy Skirlaugh."

"Skirlaugh," said Jamaica, "glad to see you too. And what brings you?"

Lavender explained why they had come and what they had brought, while they climbed from the truck and went off through the woods. Issy's head swam, and he was now only cold, even the ear was hot outside and cold in.

They came then to the bell. It was canvas, stretched on hoops of wood. A lamp inside filled it with light. In that light reality cleared the view of itself; here was how a fever felt.

This was the tent of Jamaica and Paul. Paul pulled back a flap and they went in.

Its floor was sacking and rugs. In the middle there burned a fire. Above the sides curved over but there was a wide circle open to the sky, and the smoke made its way out of that. But first it explored the tent. Issy's eyes smarted.

"We'll see to him," said Paul Paull. "What is it?"

"Shakes and burning," said Lavender. "He's Friday's lad, and we have him, and I'll explain. So we brought him to get the fever out, because he has work to do, and he belongs Friday, not us."

"We'll cure," said Jamaica. "No doubt of that." And he dug in a bag by the tent wall and brought out a handful of dry leaves, scattering them on the fire. The smoke lifted from them and began to attack Issy's eyes and throat and make him dizzy.

"Ellerby was short of the words when she ringed him," said Lavender. "I reckon."

Paul opened Issy's coat and shirt and laid a cold hand on his chest. He looked in his eyes, and at his ears. He felt the heat of the gold ring. He made a selection from leaves and twigs and roots in more bags, and put them in a pot, and the pot on the fire. He stewed them a little while, then tipped them out through a cloth, letting the liquid fall in the ashes. He squeezed the leafy stuff dry by twisting the cloth, and laid it on Issy's ear, and tied it all in place.

"That's a fit poultice," he said. "Wintergreen, willow, nettle root."

The ear went away. The whole side of Issy's head went away.

Jamaica filled the pot again, and made a dark bitter tea from herbs, and Issy had to drink that. More leaves were thrown on the fire.

"Hyssop, rue," said Paul. "Pepperwort, tansy; some to burn, some to brew. Were you ever in love yet, lad? You will be now; there's lads' love in that," and he listed the names of flowers while Issy drank two mugs of the draught. This time he went away himself, the fire and the warmth rising round him and into him, and he was being laid on the rugs on the ground so that the fire hung sideways in his mind. In his head rang names, Northumberland, Nebraska, and who was born at Greater Celandine?

Later he woke and sat up. The fire had sunk. The lamp was dark. But from outside there came light, where dawn rose under the trees. Lavender, Kingston, Paul, lay asleep about the tent, on the floor or on the cloth bags of herbs and roots.

"Time to wake," said Lavender. "You and me, Skirlaugh. You'll have to drive home, you've woken clearer than me."

"Yes, I have," said Issy. "I'm well now."

"I'm right too," said Lavender. "When you'd gone off we had a talk."

"That's it," said Paul, waking too. "Pot on for tea, Jamaica, what about it?"

"Man," said Jamaica, rising and putting the pot on the fire. "And we had some talk, right, Paull? Yes, we think we hear somewhere about the man you want. We saw him once. You want the man with the Nine Bright Shiners. You know what they say, he's the Big Wheel. But he came to us one time when he walked through a looking glass."

"Walked backwards," said Paul. "A black eye on the front, and a bruise on the backside, and looking glass in him like the crown jewels. That's the man you want."

"Shemer Burlington," said Lavender.

"Ah," said Paul, "we don't know names; we don't

know places, and if we do we don't say. We've got professional standards. All doctors have."

Issy and Lavender drank sweet herb tea, and drove back through the first of the morning.

"Tenters, those are," said Lavender, as the truck swung up a hill and set its way towards the low far thin sun. "Tenters, living out there. In the season they sell a right useless jollop to the crowds, but they can lay on a bit of good powerful fancy for their own folk. They know what to drink, eat, smoke, never a lack for them. Put you in order, haven't they?"

"Right on," said Issy. He pulled away the poultice and fingered the painless cool gold ring in his ear.

"That's my good lad," said Lavender.

At the coffle they had breakfast. Jane picked the remaining poultice leaves from Issy's ear first.

"And where next?" said Laban.

"Through the looking glass," said Lavender. "More than that we don't know."

"Don't we?" said Jane.

VII

Lall Reflects

Lall felt she had grown smaller and smaller, not by shrinking, but by having her skin peeled away, layer after layer, more and more hurt, like sweat on a blister or graze. Robert Dent had said nothing when he came to fetch her. He might as well have dropped her in his pocket, when he had asked her whether he should help her on to the coffle. When she said no he did not have any further ideas. If there was nothing to go on he would not have fancies to fill the space.

That evening he began to find out how things had been arranged. But that was when he came home. Before the day was half done Lall was sitting by Friday's fire, wondering if she had stopped shrinking and peeling. She saw quite well she could die of it, and she did not know why the coffle would send her out just to do that. She thought, after a time, when Friday sat by saying nothing, handing her cups of tea brewed on the fire, and in the little cabin of a room it was like the inside of a van, that no one in the coffle knew what they had done to her, because nothing like it had happened to them. She drank her tea, and felt happier, bit by bit. The skin grew back. And Friday was of her own people. She thought she did not want to be in that field again by herself, against that grey dying fire, in that wind between the mere and the sea.

"Was it like that for you too?" she said.

It was a short question. Ordinary people would have had to guess what Lall meant, but Friday was from the coffle and she knew.

"Worse," said Friday. "Worse and worser. I was just little, half your size, and I'd been dropped off the top of the Wheel by Shemer Burlington and I hadn't the right use of my legs, and I still haven't. One winter time the coffle came to quarters here, and they put me in the Cottage Memorial Hospital. Shemer paid up good you know; they had a court and judged it. I reckon it was worse for me than for you, with the coffle a mile away in the winter knot, and me in a great bed in a room like a field. They fixed me up, that winter, in there, but I was used to me, and didn't notice. And I got used to folk coming in each day, then going away. I wasn't big enough for them to tell me it was happening. In those days we weren't so bright. Then in the spring they told me, but I didn't hear it, maybe. They told me they were off to the gaffs again, as usual. The last I remember is my own brother, Wawne, Nazar Wawne, coming back in that room, and it wasn't very kind, but he was only a little boy, not a year older than I was, saying they'd got a better baby now, and they wouldn't see me again. So they went off and left me stretched on that bed, and there was nothing for me, they didn't have listening wireless, and they didn't have picture wireless then. And I was lying there getting older, and it came to winter again, and I was out walking a bit in the garden. That year the coffle never came. Well, I was old enough to know it wasn't true about getting a baby they liked better, but I remembered what Wawne said, and it just could be true. So the coffle didn't want me. And the hospital didn't want me either. Then Dent came in the same room. He'd got run over with a cart, and he was a sick lad, just my age. That's how I got to know him. And his mother came for him one day, and before she knew she got the pair of us, and I turned housey for a year, until the coffle came again. I forget why they missed the knot here that time. Nazar Wawne and Dent had a big tuck-up by the lake, beginning with fists, going on to levetts of wood, and finishing with brickbats, till the men dropped them both in the lake. Dent's mother sent me back to the coffle then, and so I went round for years with them, but I was never good nor use."

The rain beat against the window. The wind pulled the fire red. The kettle huffed and spat. A house could be home, Lall thought.

"What do you do?" Friday asked. "You could do a sugar barrow, I should think."

A sugar barrow is the machine that makes candy floss.

"They're thinking of getting one," said Lall.

"I couldn't do that," said Friday. "I couldn't work the treadle."

"They're electric now," said Lall. "They run off the engine."

"All that electric's invading our space," said Friday. "Well, we'll have to be around and get Dent his tea. Issy ...No, well, we have you instead."

Robert Dent did not know of the day's transaction. "So we have two of them," he said, when he came in.

"One," said Friday. "We did a fair exchange."

"Just gone away," said Robert Dent. "Has he? Do we get him back, or is it for a dozen years, like you, Denah?"

"This is a good girl, Dent," said Friday. "You always wanted a girl. And it's for while Issy has a look about for them there, like a fresh eye. Clark Riston sent him, and we can't go against that."

"Clark Riston never spoke with me," said Robert Dent. "But I know her. She's right enough. I'd like the pair, that's all. All you people act so sharp I don't know what's next because it's always past."

Later, when the day had melted behind Lall, and its sharp edges were smoothed, Friday showed her to her bed in a room above. Lall sat on the bed, in a whole room to herself, and watched Friday getting smaller down the stairs, and wondered whether it was the size and space of a house that began to shrink her again.

The next day she dared walk round to where the knot had been. There was a thin wintry sunshine, and she wore her crocheted coat with the springing-out edges. Wrapped in it, safe against being peeled by being abandoned, she walked to the ashes of the fire, and felt them still warm. It was as if the coffle had just got out of bed, so it was a pain, but not a bitter one. She left that point and went to the edge of the mere.

There she found Colin Morton standing, not watching her but keeping an eye. He had come out prepared for his swim.

"You'll be all right today?" he said. "You should be at school. Dent was at school."

"I'm all right as I am, mister," said Lall.

"What did they do?" asked Colin. "Did they leave you?"

"I got left to find out why the coffle can't go in its proper place," said Lall. "I've got to look for water, and I've got to look for something that makes certain." She thought he should be told some of these things. What he said told her what he thought, not what she should think or do.

"You don't have buildings, so it won't be that," said

Colin. "And I don't know of any. There's just one, but that wouldn't be it. You can see out on that island, just the side of a tower among the trees."

"Clark Riston didn't say it was in the water," said Lall. "And all that's standing water. He means a well or a trough."

"There's a well," said Colin. "I'll swim out, and you come in my boat, and you can see for yourself."

In the end they both went in the boat, from a landing stage by Temple Farm. "The Temple is on the island," said Colin. "I think it will be quicker if I row you out, and have my swim later." Lall hoped he would swim after she had gone. Men and women in the coffle always stayed well-covered.

The boat, a blue one, nosed in under the bare branches of a hanging willow. It bumped against a still island. "You hop out and have a look," said Colin. "I shan't row away."

"There isn't anything here, is there?" said Lall. "Animals." She looked into the stillness, like the calm of a picture of yesterday. Creatures can walk across yesterday.

"Nothing," said Colin. "Just yourself."

Lall went to look. She did not want to meet even herself; but she decided Colin meant she was the only person there.

She found more willow trees, sycamores, bramble, bracken, red berries, and startled a moorhen, which rowed away from the island at the point of its ripple.

She found a stone tower with a window, and saw the sky through the window and the top of the tower. She found the walls and fallen roof of a small building beside the tower. She bent her head and looked up the chimney and saw the same sky. Beside this fallen house she found a well, and at water-level in it, as far down as the surface of the lake, she saw sky again, and her looking head biting the circle; and when she had looked a little longer she read in the water below her own face, lit by the reflection, and stirred a little by a movement in the well.

She looked, listened, and came back to the boat. "It was not standing water," she said.

"There are springs feeding the mere," said Colin. "That is one of them. And the Temple is the only standing building I know."

"And how would they get here?" said Lall.

"That is not my problem," said Colin. He rowed her back to land. "I shall be pleased to see you any time," he said. "If I am busy I shall send you away. But I don't think you have any right to be here, you and your people. I think my cousin must be right. I think it is a pity, but facts are facts. If you are looking for a place where a building once was, look at the sheep."

"What for?" asked Lall.

"Oh, you must do some of the work," said Colin. "You watch and think. Now I am going for my swim."

Lall went away. She did not want to see him with almost nothing on. Then she thought of the baby, and walked back to Friday's house thinking of that, and not considering sheep at all.

Laban Gozzle's grey military motor bike was outside the house when she came back. Laban was inside. He was explaining how Issy had become unwell, and had been to see Jamaica Kingston and Paul Paull, with Lavender, and spent the night there. Friday was content with what he said, and knew them both. They were close kin to Lavender, who was called that from being in the flower business, the next thing to herbal medicine.

"You been here long enough, Routh?" said Laban to Lall.

"Plenty," said Lall, longing for the baby, for the crowd, for the smoke, and thinking her work done. She had looked at a well, and thought with Colin Morton that there was nothing indeed to look for. Now she wanted the ride home, wherever that was to be, on the back of the bike, her arms round her father's body.

"You've done no looking," said Friday.

"I've been out on the lake," said Lall. "With the man that let us stay the night."

"Colin Mr Morton," said Friday.

"Standing water," said Gozzle. "Isn't there more to look at than that?"

Then he had a cup of tea, rolled up a cigarette and smoked it, and said he was ready to leave. He had come up to report on Issy, and bring Lall a few more clothes.

He left without Lall. She knew she had more to do; her duty extended further. She had found out nothing so far. She had not begun to think what Colin Morton meant about the sheep. So she watched the bike thud and smoke up the lane and turn into the road, and the noise died away in the distance. She felt for a time the cold of skin dropping off again. Then she went down the lane to look for a sheep and observe it.

VIII

The Wrestlers

Issy on the back of Gozzle's bike felt it buck under his rump at the level crossing in Holderness Road. The noise fell away down the line either side as they crossed the rails, and then blurted back at him from the houses; at the crossing as if he had gone deaf, after it as if all noise were pain.

He pushed his face against Gozzle's back. The stink of the town came fully into his travel-inflated lungs, etching, itching, aching.

Gozzle's elbows moved as he held the bike to slow, between the road and the pounding crowns of the pistons, all the power and balance between his legs in the engine, between Issy's in the scything chain of the transmission.

A red light held them, a robot ray talking to the robot motor. Then the bike leapt forward again, and the town was peeled away, black, narrow, empty in the early morning. Town fell away altogether. The dwellings of the houseys began, along Anlaby Road, Hessle Road, and after the houses sky.

There was more than sky. An immense thing floated, flew, kept with them. Issy kept seeing it swim into sight and swim out. There was sky, there was water of the estuary, there was the great unknown thing, following, running ahead. Issy sat himself up to look better. The bike was running steady now, no slows, no sharp turns, no pitch and sway.

As soon as he got his head up they went pow, bash, slam, into darkness and everlasting noise. Issy thought for a moment he was dead, but the bike had gone into an underpass, a tunnel, below the ground.

In a few seconds it shook itself out again, checked, checked, checked, dropped to a crawl, so that there were separate thuds from the engine, and stopped.

"What the heck was that?" said Gozzle, and he dropped a leg to the ground. Issy felt himself as a mere weight come back to earth, unsteady on the pivot of the wheels.

"Tunnel," said Issy. It had not taken him long to realize what it was, so why should Laban Gozzle be puzzled?

"It's fresh," said Gozzle. "It was never there before. We'll have to scout a new way now; and look at that thing grown over the water."

The pursuing object was unexpected by both of them. Gozzle had often travelled the ground, but the new bridge over the estuary, flying like a bird with its towers and long deck and the hard shadow on the water below, had sprung fresh into his notion of the place, as if a hole had been burnt in the map. Then the tunnel under the access road had come as an attack. Issy did not know either this flat land and flatter water, and no dream of bridges had come to him at all.

"Well then, I wonder if they're here, that we've come to visit," said Gozzle. "With yon thing. We'll have to see."

He picked his way down a lane to the moors of the

foreshore. There the bike seemed to snuff the scent again, and harked forward along the line.

There was an encampment here below the bridge, with three or four living vans, other trailers, and a row of huts, or sheds. There were some horses picketed out. Smoke rose from a fire.

A man looked out, from the middle of the knot.

Laban Gozzle stopped the bike a hundred yards away.

"We didn't get invited," he said. "Not like the Birdman to us." With the engine stopped his voice came thin to Issy's ears. When Issy got off the bike the air came thin inside his ears; and the ground was unsettled. "And they don't care for motors," said Gozzle. "Not so very much at all. This is a different coffle, wintering here, and summering here a lot too. I don't think this spot is ever empty, always horses about. Well, they won't like that bridge. And I fancy they'll get to tell you something about Shemer Burlington."

They approached the knot. Behind the windows of the vans there was movement of women and children, looking, wary, not wanting visitors. A dog came out, bowing and smirking and waving its tail, weaving from side to side.

"We'll get bitten, I doubt," said Gozzle. "We'll not fuss."

There was a shout from the knot. Gozzle had been recognized. The dog was called back. Windows opened in the vans, and faces looked out. A greater smoke rose from the fire.

"What's this, then, Gozzle?" said a large man, wide in the shoulders, narrow at the hips, wider again at the thighs. His voice was small. "Thought you must have left home with a woman, at first."

"Friday's lad," said Gozzle. "Issy Skirlaugh. This is

Stal Ella, and here's the other one," as a second huge man came out from the knot, tucking in a shirt that scarcely went round him and just reached his waist, "Chowder Ness. Issy Skirlaugh," he finished.

"Friday's," said Stal.

"Supple enough, lingey and lish," said Chowder Ness.

"Friday got dropped off a wheel, not born like it," said Gozzle.

"Like follows like," said Chowder Ness.

They went to the knot. "I see you got a new speedway," said Gozzle, nodding towards the giant bridge walling the foreshore off.

"Can't use it," said Stal. "Pounds and pounds it costs to get on; and we don't get much into Holland."

I wonder where I go, thought Issy. It was to be Panama and Paramatta, Canton and Cape Horn; but those I have heard of: this I have not heard of; so this is stranger.

"It's a grand thing," said Chowder. "It holds the wind off us like a marvel. We should have built it ourselves."

"Damn near killed me, the road going in that tunnel under the ramp," said Gozzle. "Talk about the tunnel of love, I near choked myself with the air going solid like a wall."

They came to the fire, where sausages were cooking, and there was a sudden running of water in Issy's mouth, because nothing had been there but words and air for many hours.

They ate, they drank tea. The sun lifted in fine clouds beyond the bridge, seawards, and brought it up distinctly black with a misty light touching it and making it glitter. On it the roofs of the vehicles went by like jewels on a necklace, drawn on hidden string.

Gozzle and the two big men talked of coffles and their troubles. The big men said they had done both ill and well from the bridge contractors, even getting money from them for losing the use of some land.

"Not our land, for a kick off," said Chowder. "But good brass." No one said how much. But they had lost a useful girl to one of the cablemen: though the dog bit him, the horses kicked him and Stal and Chowder "showed him it", he had persisted, and she was on her travels. "In Holland," said Stal.

"Holland," said Issy, thinking of windmills, tiles, cheese.

"That's Holland," said Stal, pointing across the estuary. "Ness was born there. I reckon he swam here. But now you can walk back. We'd never have let her off the dry land."

After the breakfast Stal and Chowder took off their shirts. "Don't want to tear them," said Stal. They had their daily practice on the grass.

They were all-in wrestlers. In the summer season they would be in the booths of the fairgrounds, a different gaff each week. In winter they went from place to place at weekends, and their coffle watched them on television.

"Gozzle wants a go," said Stal. "Longing to put you down, Ness, take you for three submissions."

"I'll do it," said Gozzle. "Let me get stripped." He took his jacket off, and his shirt, and emptied his trouser pockets. "Bound to do it, so might as well be at it sooner," he said quietly to Issy. "They'll hurt me, but not much. I'll not fuss."

He had a wiry fight with Chowder Ness. It seemed that Chowder could have broken him at any rate, but Gozzle had sharp swift skills, and once or twice made Chowder fall over himself. Gozzle came back to the fire with a bloody nose.

"And you," said Stal to Issy.

"That's Friday's," said Gozzle. "We don't want that again, bad legs."

"Kind takes after kind," said Chowder. "That Cableman were a big lad, and our lass were a big lass."

"About Friday," said Gozzle. "We got some trouble with our winter quarters, so Clark Riston said to send this lad, Friday's lad, to find Shemer Burlington. Clark reckons he's alive."

"Be alive," said Stal. "Why not?"

"Left for dead these fifty years since," said Gozzle.

"Left *for*, not left dead," said Stal. "Eh, Chowder?"

"Shemer Burlington Holderness," said Chowder. "No need to look starey shocked, I've said nothing beyond what I can. Shemer's chief, and Shemer knows how to prove the land's yours to use. We'd no need: no one wants this place. He's chief, and he gets more than three names. He has two more, but Holderness is as far as I go."

"He's about," said Stal. "And it wasn't us left him, but our fore-elders. But whether he'll help, I can't say."

"He will," said Gozzle. "We got Nine Bright Shiners."

"You have, true?" said Stal. "Another chief? Who said? Friday?"

"Friday," said Gozzle. "Our lass Beverley had him."

"The next lass we get," said Stal, "she can be his mother, eh?"

"We'll get together on it," said Gozzle. "You listening to this, Issy? Clark Riston set you on the job."

"But where shall I look, how shall I know?" said Issy.

"Behind glass," said Chowder. "You'll tell by the Nine Bright Shiners."

"Nine Bright Shiners is luck," said Stal. "We keep the best we can, that way. Come wi' me."

He left the fireside and went across the grass, to where the horses were picketed, taking their halters one after the other, lifting them from the posts, and drawing them after him.

He had, at the end, nine of them. Then he spent half an hour trotting them round at the end of the halters, until they had worn a furrowed circle on the grass. He halted them, spoke to each one, and took the halters from their bridles. He gave them the word to start trotting again, and they obediently circled, looking with cautious eye each at Stal and Issy in the middle of the ring.

Beyond them the bridge was a brooch against the sky.

"Now hee-up," said Stal, and the trotting stopped. All the horses turned inwards, like the spokes of a wheel, reared, and for a moment stood on their hind legs, so that Issy had to look up. When he did he saw the nine dark heads, and on each brow the white blaze of a star, the Nine Bright Shiners belonging to this knot, ringing him.

"We are the people that invented the wheel," said Stal. "And don't forget it. We brought it to the world."

And later, much later, when the sun had swung over the bridge and fallen into the mists of the western river, and the sky came up clear, and the bridge grew quiet and invisible but for the red lamps on the towers, Chowder began to show the stars, circling the heavens. The red lights of the bridge, and the glow of the town grew to be petty gleams indeed as Issy watched with him. Under Chowder's instruction he found, saw, and understood the Nine Bright Shiners of the sky, with the four corner stars of the rim, and the five of the felly, what other men call Orion, but the people of the coffle call the Lesser Wheel. The Great Wheel, said Chowder, was not in view tonight.

But what they saw was the sign and arrangement on the baby's back.

"That is what you look for," said Stal. "You'll not see it direct, I dare say; there'll be something between. But what he'll do I can't say. What he'll do," and he shook his head and shrugged the muscles of his shoulders.

Issy and Gozzle walked to the bike, and blasted their way through the tunnel, through the darkness, through the fixed stars, back to the knot by the mouth of the estuary, like some rocket.

IX

The Great Wheel

Rain was falling in a distant way, as if it did not reach the roof above Lall's head. Instead of having the top of the living van sounding at every drop, there was the space of loft and the thick of tiles to muffle the sound.

But there was real rain falling, and outside, when Lall pushed the window open, and cold water ran down her hand, the rain hissed and sang in the grass, and great drops slapped the road, cratering the pools standing there.

Downstairs, when Lall sat with Friday, with Robert Dent long gone wet to work ("It's a job to remember who I'm leaving, you two lasses"), the drops came plump down the chimney and danced dry in the fire. They splashed down on the path outside the door, jumping on the rebound over the threshold, and running across the floor and under the rug.

"Can't still bear a shut door," said Friday. "I was brought up in an old van, and I never got cosy. But a van is different, up the steps, and you don't get the water running in like that."

The fire darkened down when rain and soot fell on it, then glowed again. It smelt all at once like the steam engine. For a moment Lall was back in the coffle, and then was not. She wanted urgently to go and handle the baby, to look at it, to pick it up, to see the day in its eyes. But it could not be. Instead of it there was nothing, a missing step.

"You'll want breakfast," said Friday.

Lall had been here a week. She was fully settled, she thought, if she looked at herself without thinking how she felt about it. She knew what shops to go to, where to put the provisions she and Friday bought, what to cook with. She knew her way about, without finding anywhere to go, or anyone to be. Robert Dent looked at her, from time to time, and thought she was Issy, changed, not her own self as she knew it.

This day was the worst for rain, but not the first. On a fine day Lavender had come back, driving the little truck, and taken her off to his field at Skipsea. It was a field where horses once had kept, and where his mother had grown her lavender, that he was named after. There was still a bank of it by the gateway, with nothing gathered from it, the stalks dead and bare. The field itself was let to a farmer, and was ploughed and harrowed flat, and a green thing growing.

"That's that," said Lavender. "Winter wheat. I thought we might have got on here for a day or two. But I can't say anything about that. No good here. We'll go on to Rickle Pits or Emmotland, and see what we can do there."

Rickle Pits and Emmotland were no help, with shook heads and hands dried on aprons at kitchen doors, saying it can't be done these days.

"We'll have to frog around the south coast," said Lavender. "I believe they don't want us there, but there's places along the tide we can be in for a while before they send us on. The trouble is, we don't get to put the shows up and paint and mend, which is what

God designed winter for. We know we should be at Burton, by rights."

"I didn't find anything," said Lall.

All she had so far done was look at a temple on an island, and she was not troubling to explain about that, because it was not worth explaining. No island was useful to the coffle.

But Lavender was, at the same time as she was running that through her mind, beginning to talk about sunken islands off the south coast, where they could have been content, wintering among the surfs of the estuary.

Back at Burton again Lavender drove down past Colin Morton's farm, and parked by the wet ash of the fire. He walked to the hedge and looked over.

"That's where we were," he said. "In other years. Laban says it's true we can't go in there. So you go on looking, Lall, and you'll see it, somehow."

Lall had not seen. She had stayed by the fireside on the wet days, and done less than her duty.

The steady rain of the worst day stopped about two o'clock, and a blue sky pushed through the clouds. The sun stayed behind a cloud, putting down a leg of light that walked over fields and buildings and trees to the south of the town.

Lall went out then, and wandered in a cool brightness by the edge of the mere, past where the knot had been, along the waterside where the grass was covered with rising mere and the little sandy banks were lost.

She went through a hedge to get into the next field. It was grass again, and not a planted crop. There were sheep in it, looking at her down their noses; and eating. Lall had a fancy that they were really people, houseys of a very elementary sort.

But there was a little house, by the far hedge. Lall

made her way to it. Its door was in the next field, and she had to go a long way about to get through to it, climbing over barbed wire.

The little hut had a door, which opened, and a hole in the roof. But dry inside was a heap of sacks, and some rusty farming implements, some bags of farm powders. There was a red-stained kettle, sitting on an iron stove. Everything iron was rusty, everything plastic was dusty, all the cloth sacks were musty.

Lall felt the keen silence of the day, the fields, go away a little. She felt that this hut was her own lair, her own place. It was here she could come, she felt, to look at the land; this would be her knot; she would be the coffle of this field. Now she knew her way about, and had somewhere to go. Now she was not tied to Friday.

With sacks above and sacks below she could sleep; with fire in the little stove she could live.

Selmah's baby would have enjoyed it here too, perhaps.

She fell to thinking about the baby, and began to model without intention a sacking doll, tied and torn, burlap-faced, jute-legged, a fancied smile, remembered eyes with no true day in them, a weight to hold, a shape to nurse, not real, but filling a space.

She sat until twilight, cold, but warm with finding she knew where she was. Then, as stars came out, she put the booby of a doll under the sacks without ceremony or goodnight – it was not a toy for a child looking to the future, but something for her past, for what she had lost, not for play, but to fill emptiness.

She took herself away. Now she felt the contentment of finding a place to be, now she was better off than Lavender and Laban and the rest of the coffle. She had found her island; she had her winter quarters where she could be familiar with herself, where, if she had them, she could put up her rides and booths and paint them all winter long. She thought of herself with a sugar barrow handing out pink bundles of floss to wild sheep. A booby baby would watch. Lall, feeling these thoughts strange, knowing she was not thinking them, ran herself away from them, towards Friday's house; home.

The next day she took firing for the little stove. She watched the wood to ashes, and the ash to smoke, and felt a little warm. But all the heat went out of the hole in the roof. She dipped the red cast-iron kettle in the lake, and could hardly carry it back. She stood it on the stove. The fire died below it. Lall left it and went to look at what new domains she now had, to see what place this was the centre of.

One field is like another. Some have sheep in, some young bullocks; grass is grass and waterside is that or mud. Somewhere round the end of the mere there was a little road down, and a parking place for sailing boats, with tall dead stems of the stuff called kelk growing between the hulls like extra masts. The wind blew through and the wire stays and shrouds rattled busy.

Lall left that strange crop. She crossed a little stream, where water ran from mere to sea, and came upon more fields. A notice on a gate said, "Burton Farms Limited. Private. Keep Out." It was a strip of turnipy ground. She climbed the gate and crossed among the turnips.

Beyond them the hedge was different. Lall thought she could tell that she was no longer in Burton Farms Limited. Their hedges, cut by Robert Dent, were neat and mended. The ones she now saw had been let go, and were wild and wide. There was a path through, where sheep had been coming to steal the turnipy crop. A net of wire was across it, and Lall stepped over that.

In the field beyond were sheep, lying down and chewing, up the middle of the field.

This row of moving jaws, all turned towards her, reminded her of eating. The sheep were eating grass, or perhaps turnips. Lall recollected stew at Friday's, and came away.

A sensible instinct told her that she was much nearer home than the way she had come. She followed up the little lane by the rattling boats, and came into the road, turned left, and was soon at Friday's house. She had come in a small circle, with a fireplace at each end of a line across it, because, when she worked it out, the hut she had found was little more than a field from Friday's garden. However, it was a world off in other ways.

She went to it the next day, taking her dinner with her in a paper bag, as Robert Dent often took his. From it, when she looked, she could see Friday's house. Of course, in this direction she could not get further away, because the mere was the next thing.

The third or fourth day, while she was busy house-keeping the stove, and while she wondered whether the doll thought of her any more, or she of it, she heard something approach, nearer than she liked. It was a tractor, driven by Edwin Barker, of Burton Farms Limited. Its destination was the hut. Lall saw from the little window in the door.

Then she had one foot on the stove, another on the wall, and was out through the hole in the roof. Before she leapt she stowed the doll in its sleeping place, surely and for ever ashamed of it. But her dinner stayed in its brown paper bag on the heap of sacks. She jumped down behind the hut while someone came in and went out, and the tractor left. She watched it go out of the field, one man driving, another riding behind. When she went round to the front of the hut again she found it padlocked.

Now she was homeless again. And for the time being

she was dinnerless. She went back to the house, and there was Robert Dent eating his dinner. On the table, beside Lall's place, was the paper bag with hers in it.

"I didn't say anything," said Robert Dent, looking up from his knife, "but I know a paper bag when I see it. You don't want to be there. I reckon your place isn't on Burton Farms. You'll want to be round the corner a bit, if it's anywhere. And you don't want broth of that kettle – that's sheep raddle, that is; we mark them red with it."

Lall opened the bag and ate her cheese sandwich. There was nothing else to be done. "Is it poison?" she asked.

"Don't kill sheep," said Robert Dent. "But they don't sup it."

"You want to ask that Colin Mr Morton," said Friday. "If he doesn't know, he'll still tell you, he's clever enough."

"He told me to look at sheep," said Lall. "Watch them."

"Remarkable things, sheep," said Robert Dent. "Plenty of them to watch about here. You want to know about land, ask a sheep. They know, but they can't tell."

"I'll make them," said Lall. She wondered how the sheep would respond. "So far they haven't been worth the watch I've given them."

"Like a turnip watch," said Robert Dent. "Eh?"

That evening, though, when night came on, and there was neither cloud nor wind, and nothing moved unless it wanted, Lall did want, and went out, charmed by the still cold.

Overhead was the gallery of star pictures, each punched out distinct, each clearly at a different distance. And each, somehow, should be numbered, so that the points could be joined up. She went inside to say something of this to Friday, because she knew the stars were known by her people. Friday came outside to look with her.

"There's the one that's ours," she said. "We invented the wheel, and there it is, the Lesser Wheel, but some call it Orion, housey people call it something like that as well."

"I didn't know we could use that word," said Lall, because there were reasons for not saying it.

"You'll see," said Friday. "Now see the Great Wheel," and she showed Lall the great curve of the Milky Way, and they walked down to the gate in the lane, following it, and saw it stand above the calm mere, reflected upright in it, one end in heaven, the other in earth, below the water. Lall, seeing it, remembered the line of chewing sheep across a field, and knew she had been told something by them. She resolved too, that she would seek now until she found: the sooner she did the sooner she could join the coffle and Selmah's real baby.

There was a pang about leaving the musty sack-cloth one; but it knew no better.

A further thought came, that finding what she had to find was important beyond the baby and what she felt for it. Neither it nor the toy of it was hers, in any case.

Later on Robert Dent said, "You can have a moppet out of the market, you want it, Lall. I wondered when I saw it, thinking Issy has changed proper, because he would, if he had."

"He hasn't," said Lall. "I don't want one, Dent. I left it behind."

"Dinner too," said Robert Dent. "You want a thing, you say, along of you are here, eh?"

X

World's End

Land went. Water swelled up beside the steam engine, rising on the driving wheels, spraying up the front ones, kissing the cleated iron tires as they went through it. Everything solid narrowed down to the road.

And there was nothing ahead. The road faded, but in a way that made it seem that vision had gone wrong, because the engine used the road up and there was still some more.

"Nothing behind, either," said Lavender.

There was nothing behind. They had left the real fields and come on to the narrow promontory, road-wide at high water, and now those real fields were beyond sight.

"Misty," said Issy. "Roky."

"Cold and all," said Lavender, slowing the engine. "Not much to see out here," he said.

The water was disappearing, though it was still there, certainly, beyond sight, but lifting from either wheel. They were awash, at sea. On either side, ahead and behind, nothing could be seen.

"We want navigation lights," said Lavender. The engine's canopy was strung with coloured bulbs, but without the generator, which lived separately and was driven by a belt, they could not light up.

Seaweed climbed up the right-hand wheel, and went over the top.

"We've gone off the edge of the beach," said Issy, his voice crowing a little with worry.

"Swim back," said Lavender. "No we haven't. It's the tide over the causey. We're not in that deep. We're on hard road. There's often dry land ahead."

"Often?" said Issy.

"Been known," said Lavender.

There was a great PHAAAAP from a foghorn bellowing in the fog. Issy thought it was a ship, and that they were truly at sea and about to be run down.

"Could be," said Lavender. "It's been done along here. I remember once there was some stuff to be got out of a ship that landed where it shouldn't. Don't worrit. We're on the road, even if we can't see it."

PHAAAAP, went the foghorn.

"We'll follow on that," said Lavender. "It won't be simpler, it can't be. Ships steer off; we steer on."

Further away a vessel hooted, and another seemed to echo. More distantly still the Bull Lightship called and called.

Lavender blew the whistle of the engine. "We're at sea," he said. "Steamer, we are."

Water washed below, milled by the wheels, reaching the perch, slapping at the bottom of the fire, stinking.

"Salt as herring," said Lavender, "and all to wash off after."

They groped ahead for ten minutes. To Issy nothing changed outside. There was still the bright curdle of fog, no object showing, no actuality present. And four times the foghorn went PHAAAP ahead of them, and each time Issy replied, when Lavender gave him the cord.

The noise the wheels made altered from pumping and paddling to grinding and groping. "Out of the water," said Lavender. "Where do you think we got to? Holland?"

Issy did not know. Out of the water would do.

There was another change soon. The noise of the engine had been flowing out through their surroundings, lost in the fog. There was now a sort of echo, a reflection. First it had delay, and then it came at the same time as the noise. Shadows stood in the mist. They were among houses.

"Got to town," said Lavender.

There was a great rounded wall, which they drove about, Lavender swinging the wheel. "Lighthouse," he said.

They left the houses. They left the road. The road was the only real thing, Issy found, when they no longer had it and were on loose sand.

"Steady," said Lavender, to the engine, feeling the sand settle under the wheels.

"Don't you think we've got there?" said Issy.

"Well," said Lavender, "I'm not sure which way round we are, going about the lighthouse, and going on might take us back. We'll get out and shout."

The foghorn shouted first. It gave them no direction, sounding overhead; as if they were underwater, Issy thought.

Lavender got down and started calling, like some strange dream, for fish: "Fish, Fish," he called. Then, oddly, "Swine, Swine. Give a hoot, Issy."

Issy pulled the whistle cord.

PHAAAP, said the foghorn, in immediate reply.

Lavender changed his tune, and called for Honey, and then for a meaningless word, Strunch.

They were the names of people, who came bulking out of the vapours to them before long, and stood looking to see who had called, at what iron thing had lumbered across water to them, the elephant, the mammoth, of transport, standing on the sand in the fog, unlit, unlooking.

Fish Swine was a man with a great caved-in long face and huge eyes bedded in a beach of wrinkles. Honey Strunch was a woman, in a black dress like Ellerby's or the other women's, a check apron, a round face with no large feature, but tense brown eyes that Issy could see himself in, and Lavender, and a great banded thing close against them. He thought that was part of the eye, but he felt something stroke him. Looking round, wondering, he saw the lighthouse clear of mist standing tall into a blue sky. The sunlight climbed on it and walked on him.

They were all on the end of some island, he saw as the mist cleared away and the sunshine came down to the water. To one side was sea, to the other the estuary, and between, to the south, the further shore of British Holland, where you could walk the long way.

On this island, though it was no island if the road came here, stood the lighthouse, a house or two more, and a small knot from a tiny coffle. There were two living vans and two exhibition vans, wintering here in the eye of the sea. Round them stretched dunes of sand, with crowns of weary grass, clinging and sparse.

"A plenty of driftwood, if you'll take some back," Fish Swine was saying.

"I'll load some," said Lavender. "There isn't plenty of room on an engine. You talk to this lad of Friday's, looking for Shemer Burlington, he is, on Clark Riston's say, because we got turned off at Burton."

"That spot you were in," said Fish Swine, "you can't talk back about. But Clark's right. You'd best hear from Shemer."

"But where is he?" said Issy.

"Ah," said Honey Strunch. "He's where you might think of looking, if you wanted to, in a manner of speaking."

"But it's not for us to say," said Fish.

"And we haven't the knowing," said Lavender.

"Ah," said Fish, "those long times past, when we had a big knot at Burton. When I was a little lad, before it went wrong."

"Before that," said Honey. "And how's Friday, then? Is she getting about?"

Issy answered questions. Then Honey went to her fire among the vans and trailers and began cooking. In the vans was a tribe of children, who spent their time taking quick looks at Issy, and then looking away, steadily. They did nothing else but look the other way, apart from their glances towards him. It was work for them.

Fish took Issy to the exhibition trailers. The children melted away before him, unlooking, unseeing.

"Get and help Strunch," said Fish sharply, but the children looked up, looked down, and always away. "Miserable spot this, and miserable whelps," said Fish. "Spawn."

He took Issy into a warm trailer. He left him in a bare room with dark windows, and went beyond, striking matches. As he did so Issy saw light come through the windows, and discovered they were fish tanks, and swimming in the clear water the little fish, transparent to the light beyond with fin and swirling tail, hanging like gold and silver coins in the water, reflecting, refracting, silhouette and shape, individual in outline, in their small gatherings making patterns.

"What else do you know?" said Fish. "Of Shemer."

"See him behind glass," said Issy. "Like fishes, eh?"

"Here are fishes," said Fish. "Shemer isn't here.

You'll have to look further. But it was a shameful thing they did for him; but you'll know all that, with how he dealt with your own mother. I reckon they should have joined in mending that accident and kept all together. Shemer was the chief, and still is, or we'd have heard. But he owes nothing to us now, and might not want to know you."

"But what of the glass?" said Issy.

"Ah," said Fish, "I think you won't see him. You come and look at my glass, and my fishes. But you'll want Shemer, so you have to do the best, and you have to tell him what your people won't say, how they want to make amends and forget old scores, if he will. Shemer holds the proof. They couldn't take the Nine Bright Shiners from him, and they couldn't take his chieftaincy. If he's kept his papers these fifty years you might come right. And we'll be at Burton too. We don't want to be in this miserable place each winter for ever, nigh on needing a lifeboat to get to the toilet."

Issy saw the fish in both trailers. Fish had to put on his exhibition voice and manners for him, as if he were a crowd come in and paying.

"And this," said Fish, "is the Immortal Guppy, what wrote his life story, and if you don't believe, just go down to the public library, yes madam, library, and ask for the book, the Immortal Guppy wrote it. And here a descendent of the national royal house of Japan, the Mitsubishi Shubunkin, in full colour, no licence needed, smuggled out of Tokyo by Marco Polo the Peppermint King, very simple, he filled the hole with water. And this tank you won't see the like of anywhere. I won't tap the glass, it disturbs the fish. These are the original Sumatran Invisible Fish, and I had three this morning, but as you can tell there are now four, another one has hatched, what a sight, absolutely transparent except when they close their eyes, very rare. You get a better view if you close yours, that's it, young woman. You understand, you are invisible to them when you have your eyes open. So blink gently."

There was the Somersaulting Mussel, sitting in the mud of a tank and turning over when Fish tapped the glass. "That's genuine," he said. "I trained it myself. But it's different for this," and he showed Issy a trap-door with water below. "We say it's sharks," he said, and poked in a stick. "It's easy in a crowd." He kicked on a small lever, and there was a snapping sound and the stick was broken under the water. A triangle, like a shark's fin came up, swam across, and sank again. "Then I trip and put my foot in, and they help me out," he said. "We go round the block, past the crabs and eels, and come back, and I take the lid off again and it's the Atlantic Dolphin, and I whistle for it but it won't come, so we give up waiting, and all at once ... " and there was a swirl in the water, where a smiling dolphin reared up, painted to be better than life, said "Good day", and plunged under again, making a tremendous splash. "Then I get them to throw money in, and if they put in enough he comes out again, and the wetter they get the more they enjoy it. That's houseys for you."

Last of all he showed his private collection, of nine starfish. They were, he said, his Nine Bright Shiners. And after that Honey called them to eat, among the shy children with their backs to him, eating like cats.

"It isn't the greatest show on earth, like," said Lavender on the way back.

"I'll say," said Issy.

"Don't get particular, young Skirlaugh," said Lavender.

Young Skirlaugh wished he stayed, though, not for the fish or the strange children, but because he filled the day of his mind with coming through the water (Cape Horn overland?) high on the steam engine; with bright lamps on the canopy at the sea's utter edge, and beyond, three parts of the world water; with replying to the fog's hard cry by a steamy, fog-breeding whistle. The thought floated in and out of his mind, coloured like a bird, leisurely as a fish.

"Wake up," said Lavender. "I want to be at the coals under your backside."

XI

A Sign on the Ground

Lall went one fine winter Thursday to Driffield Mart with Robert Dent, who was taking a wagonload of fat bullocks from Burton Farms Limited.

Lall was longing for a ride. She would have gone without longing, because she had more need than most to see further and often. She had been brought up travelling, and always, everywhere she looked, it was the next place she saw, not what stood round her.

Being still discontented her, though apart from missing the baby, she liked very much living with Friday, day and night; she loved her own steady bed and the stiff stair that led to it; she breathed deeper and moved better indoors, with more space to do it in. She could stay dry on a wet day without feeling cramped. And the quiet of having no neighbour five feet away was soothing, though what needed soothing she could not tell; but no one had quarrelled round her since she came here.

For all that she still had to be afoot and in fresh places to feel complete.

Dent picked her up at the door of the house, and she was up high on the plastic seat and moving along the road, and watching, looking. Her eyes drank the road, her mind breathed it, and her heart set its teeth in all she saw.

"Sit stiller," said Robert Dent. "You've revived up."

"I know," said Lall, and she counted her money.

"Not much of a buying spot, Driffield, maybe," said Robert Dent. "But if you fancy a cow we could bring it back with us, no trouble about that."

"Might get a sheep," said Lall, though she intended nothing of the sort. Now she sat twitching with excitement, more than before the journey began, wanting to hurry along and yet lengthen the distance; wanting to travel for ever yet be there at once.

They ran into Driffield. Robert Dent put Lall down at the street market, telling her where to be, and when. She got down on to the unexplored cobbles, feeling as Issy would feel if he reached veritable Katmandu (but without knowing what Issy might think about anything). For Lall the feeling was splendid; she was at home in strange lands.

In a corner of the market she found Liz Carnaby, selling bolt ends, remnants, and rag bundles. Liz had married out of the coffle and then come back to trade on her own. She sold all the year round in different markets day after day, cycling between gaffs on a three-wheeler with a trailer.

"Now then, Routh," she said as soon as she saw Lall, "come back here and help; there's little trade today," and she was digging in her bowl of cold money to send Lall for cups of tea, "trade price, mind."

Lall had everything that day, the new, the needed, the known; she was out and in to just the comfortable degree. She had her cup of tea with Liz, rolled up cloth for her, minded the stall for a time while Liz went on a flight round the cobbles, had her dinner of a hot dog and chips with relish, talked to Liz after it of the coffle's doings ("Aye," said Liz, "you get off the moving thing when you go in a house; and it's that thing that drives you, and maybe you should drive yourself; so I wonder"); and the Nine Bright Shiners ("Summat and nowt," said Liz. "Nowt and summat; but there, I reckon it's gone, all that; Shemer is the last one, and when it comes to it he'll be buried and forgotten: we folk don't get buried if we do it right, and a chief never: I heard the place for laying a chief down is at Burton; and for Shemer it's said to be the van where they left him, or the like of it; and they haven't forgot in the coffle, but they won't remember for all that"); and the exchange she had made with Issy ("Friday's child," said Liz; "take Friday this bolt end, will it do?"); and the task of finding each of them had, and was at the appointed place for Robert Dent and the wagon when the time came.

"Did you get done?" said Robert Dent.

"Aye, and plenty," said Lall.

"Been buying," said Robert Dent, looking at the bolt end still on its board.

"Liz Carnaby sent it," said Lall.

"There's this and that," said Robert Dent, and he hauled up from the floor a sacking bag with a grinning pig's head in it.

Lall spent the next days in peace with her surroundings and glad to be at rest. She helped to salt the pig's head, and to lay out the bolt end for sewing.

She wandered in the fields again, wondering what sheep could tell her, their heads mopping at the grass or fixed towards her in a connected gaze. She had been told something, she knew, when the long line had formed as the sheep lay across a field.

"Not our field," said Robert Dent. "That belongs Wassand, or they have use of it. You want to go there and ask them. But there's nothing there, lass."

"Just these sheep acting funny," said Lall.

She went there again, and yet again. The sheep were walking, standing, in clumps, scattered, lying at random. She could see no code in their movements, no cipher in their arrangement, no words in their occupations, no message in their activity. She herself added a punctuation to the meaningless sentence by standing in the corner of the field in dry days and on a rustling carpet of frost, while wrens flew about the hedge and bluetits scolded, and she heard the grass tear in sheep teeth. She became very bored with that and went home.

She met Colin Morton in the street one day.

"School time," he said. "Where you should be."

"I don't live here," said Lall. "I'm just visiting my auntie."

"She should take you along there," said Colin.

Lall turned aside and went into a shop. Colin went on towards his house.

Lall did her shopping and followed him. She was not prepared to ask him questions in the street, but thought she could at his house. Houseys were different in their homes, Jane always said. They would buy things to make you go away, so home was where you did best, if you were selling. Laban had said that that was gypsy talk, and Ellerby said no more, particular about not being a gypsy, even if she sold like one in hard times.

Colin knew he was being followed. He waited for Lall at his garden gate. "Anything from the sheep?" he said. "I've seen you watching them. Or do you want to go to school?"

"I saw them once lying in a long line, like the Great Wheel," said Lall.

"The Great Wheel?" said Colin. "What's that?"

Lall looked up at the sky, but it was broad daylight,

and cloudy too. No doubt the stars were there, but certainly invisible. "It's the Milky Way," she said.

"Well, I suppose it rains up there too," said Colin. "Is that any help?"

"It's daft lot of help," said Lall. "Is that some school learning?"

"I don't have much to do," said Colin. "I trained for a school teacher and there isn't any work. So I've plenty of time. And I just noticed that sheep like to lie in a dry place. They don't teach you that in school, I know."

"You don't have to be a sheep to lie in a dry place," said Lall. "I'd know it myself."

"If you watch them," said Colin, "you can find which the dry places are."

"It's where the sheep are lying," said Lall.

"Don't get pert," said Colin. "You're just being the clever monkey."

"Have a crisp," said Lall, because that was what she had bought when she went into the shop, and now she wanted not to offend.

"Thanks," said Colin. "But the next question is, why is the ground dry just there?"

"Because that's where the sheep is lying," said Lall. "But that can't be just it, eh?"

"No," said Colin. "Down in that pasture where you camped that night there used to be a building that got pulled down. Well, I've often seen sheep lie just in the pattern of that building, where the foundation is with the grass growing over it."

"Maybe they remember the building and think they're in it," said Lall. "Another crisp?"

"No, thanks," said Colin. "They're lying on the foundation, because that is dryer; and I think it will feel warmer to them. So where you were watching, maybe you saw something. You'll want wet weather, then they'll find the dry again."

"Right," said Lall. "Now you've eaten all the crisps. But that field, Dent doesn't know who it belongs to, and Friday thought you might."

"It belongs to someone who lives away," said Colin. "Somebody called Ryan, lives in Hull. Burton Farms want to buy it, and so do they at Wassand. Now, if you went to school it would be dinner time, so I'm going for mine. You watch the sheep, and you might find."

"Might, eh?" said Lall, licking the salt from the inside of the crisp bag.

She went back to the house. In the afternoon she went out and looked at the field beyond the little stream, beyond the turnips. She could see the place where her own feet had trampled as she watched on other days.

She went through the sheep like a drop of oil on water, repelling a circle of them round her, like some feared shepherd.

She stood near the middle of the field, looked at by eyes, unlooked at by the winter country. Where, she thought, would a coffle of sheep make its knot? Was there any warmth at all in any of the ground; was there any difference? If a sheep could speak would it tell where the Great Wheel lay, where the Milky Way? This can't be me thinking about things. Thinking is very foolish and hurts my head at the front.

A sheep spoke, as if it were willing to help but did not know the language. A black bird flew overhead.

When Lall came to the place she saw where the sheep had been lying. There were stones showing through the grass, dry as the weather, damp as the air. Along and across the field there seemed to have been a wall, now gone.

It is nothing to do with the sheep, Lall thought; Colin Mr Morton knows it is like this. But houseys always speak round corners, not straight out. And he had not told all, she was sure.

He had not, indeed.

In the middle of the field were stone slabs, set not quite level, and lapped by a line of other slabs down the middle, like a little wall, reminiscent of something. It joined the wall of the Milky Way, which ran up to it, kept the wall at the centre, had nettle stalks, sprouted a thorny bush, grew a willowy tree, widened to the slabs, dropped down a steep little slope, and died away in the other half of the field. A deaf old sheep, sitting chewing down the slope, trotted away with a reproachful, mouthful, bleat.

For the moment Lall saw nothing, no building, no roof. She had the dry line of the field, and something of its reason, but no more. To her there was no building.

She found she was cold, and knew that nothing was being told to her, even after the useful-sounding words of Colin Morton.

She went home to Friday's house in the failing light. Friday was glowing up the fire, boiling the kettle, and wondering where Issy was, what he was doing. Lall sat by the fire and wondered about the baby, and what it was doing and whether it would ever see her again. Then Friday brewed tea, and Lall made toast, which they had with butter and jam, and the last of the light seeped into the cracks between the floorboards and between the square sections of the ceiling. Only the fire gave any light now. The frost began to scratch at the window.

"Like in a trailer," said Friday. "When I first came in Burton in the coffle we were the first to have electric to see by. We got it before the houseys, off the steam engine. Folk used to visit our stately home. And there's only coffle people without it now, like Fish at Spurn, and Stal at Ferriby, lurking away with oil lamps. But before that even. well, we had the fire to light us of a night, in the middle of the knot, and maybe a little stove in the van."

And Lall, looking up at the dark ceiling, saw that the squares of it were stone, and that she had walked on stone, stone that was the roof of a dwelling, out in the fields, along the Great Wheel, the Milky Way.

XII

The Wheelwright

It was Robert Dent who thought the bus to Hull was the bus to nowhere. But he came down on it and met Issy there, to look at him.

"Well, I don't like the town," he said. "And what like is it with so many of those folk, Issy?"

"Right enough," said Issy. "I've met plenty of them."

"I was used to just one," said Robert Dent. "And now I have two. The little one clatters on. She hadn't much to say at first, but they both know places I've not heard of. So do you, I daresay."

But not Ulan Bator, Trincomalee, and Dallas, Texas, thought Issy. Perhaps no one goes to famous places, only to Withernwick, Sunk Island, or Sproatley.

"York Abbey and such," said Robert Dent. "Now I'll set off back."

They were having a cup of tea at the bus station. Robert Dent got back on the bus he had left half an hour before. He said he was enjoying his journey. Issy watched the bus leave.

When he turned to walk back to Laban's bike he was stopped by Jamaica Kingston.

"This way, man," said Kingston.

"I'm with Laban," said Issy.

"I know, man," said Kingston. "But this way."

Kingston's way was through streets and courts, alleys and avenues, all under a wind that came from the east and cut thin slices from Issy's face. Hurrying into it squeezed water from his eyes, into the corners and down his jaw. Kingston kept an impelling hand just below his shoulders, pressing him along. He was crushed between wind and fist.

They came to the river, that same estuary, grey and oily against the quays, slapping cold against the concrete walls, picking and hissing against wooden piles, fourteen, twenty feet below.

They passed along this dry wharf and along the ten-foots between the terraces, inland again. In a farther street were wintry afternoon shops. Beyond them lay a dump, lorry tyres piled high beyond the fence, the corpses of cars stacked in a mass grave, the rusting girders of other broken things tangled and dismantled, ripped and ruined, pointing to the grey sky.

Beyond the dump, behind a similar fence, was an area that seemed to have nothing in it. The gaps in the fence let through vertical landscapes of dry weeds, the scrap of nature's summer, riveted rusty dock, unpolished grass heads, the black head bones of hogweed, the kelk.

There were double gates. In one was set a small door. Beside the door was the little button of a door bell, a small light glowing from it.

"You push that," said Kingston.

Issy pushed it. No bell sounded for him.

"Way back in," said Kingston.

Footsteps sounded beyond the gates. There was a small scratching noise. Issy was sure he was being looked at through a spyhole. He tried to look as if he knew what he was doing here.

"Jamaica Kingston and Issachar Skirlaugh," said Kingston loudly. "Me, and him; him and me."

There was a set of short, loud scraping noises. It was the noise of bolts being drawn back, three of them.

"We get in, man," said Kingston.

The footsteps beyond the gate went away. Kingston pushed at the small door. It was still fast in the larger one. He tried both larger doors, but they were solid too.

"He bolted them against us," said Kingston. "He never undid them at all."

"Who?" said Issy.

"We all know, we all can't say," said Kingston. He rang the bell again. This time nothing happened at all.

Far down the vacant field beyond the gate there were noises now, of thick wooden poles being moved, dropped, rolled.

"He won't open for me," said Kingston. "But I wonder what he's doing."

"Who?" said Issy. "Who is it?"

"You'll find, man," said Kingston. "Now you'd better be off. Gozzle will be waiting of you."

Issy found his own way back, because Kingston loped off in a way that was not meant to be followed, out of sight. Issy had to wait by the bike for the best part of an hour, before Laban turned up.

"You'll have to try again," Laban said, and kicked the bike to life. Issy sat with his face sheltered and the wind ripped flesh from his bones, and whistled through his skeleton. Graveyard, Issy thought, Iguanodon, Fossil Remains thirty miles. It must be Shemer walking behind the fence. And my hands have now fallen off.

Jane Ellerby sat him and Gozzle against the fire when they got back. "The further and faster you go the colder and more starved you get," she said.

"He's getting warmer, is Skirlaugh," said Laban.

Some days later, in the same wind, Issy went more comfortably into Hull with Lavender, in the small truck.

They parked by the wintry shops. "I'm saying nothing," said Lavender. He had said the same all the way in. "How can I know anything? I know nowt."

There was the same dump. Nothing had changed there. Beyond there was the same fence with the decaying field behind it, the tall cracks in the fence showing the tall stalks. The stalks swayed; the fence itself leaned back and forth in the wind.

But there was a change in the field. Beyond the grass there was a heap of things that had not been there before, and beyond the heap an array of posts, taller than the grass and more regular, not moving.

The wind blew bitterly through the cracks. It was impossible to stand and look.

Lavender took Issy to the first of the cracks, and then turned back. "I'll be at the truck," he said. "Bit of shopping to do." And he left.

Coming from the other direction were two people. Issy watched Lavender go towards the shops. Issy knew he was never going shopping. Issy turned and saw the two behind him coming nearer.

"We're waiting of you," said the man. It was Fish, and the woman was Honey Strunch. Her coat had a double row of silvery buttons, down the front and down the back. There was something about her that reminded Issy of Friday. Fish wore a best blue suit and had a red scarf coiled round his neck.

"Last time I rang the bell," said Issy. "I don't know why."

"You will when he answers," said Fish.

"If he does," said Honey. "I'm sure I wish he would."

Issy pressed the bell beside the small door let into the larger gate.

Again someone the other side walked to the door. Again Issy felt he was being looked at. Again bolts were drawn, but whether they were drawn closed or drawn open could not be told.

Again the feet walked away.

"Wait," said Fish, when Issy would have gone to push at the door.

Issy waited. Somewhere down in the field he heard a mallet striking wood, a post being driven in, the note of the struck pole climbing higher as the post shortened.

Fish let him try the gate. It was still hard shut.

Fish and Honey stood back from the fence and let their eyes see through the cracks in it. Issy stood with them, looked with them. They understood what they saw, looking at each and nodding and being satisfied. Issy could make nothing of it. Something was being constructed.

"What's he making?" he said, thinking of Ararat, Ravenserodd, Lyonesse, all floods and Arks. "Shemer," he said, thinking of Noah.

"Wheelwright," said Fish. "He'll make anything."

"He's here," said Issy. It was a question.

"Nobody answered the bell," said Fish. "Invisible man. Close your eyes, then he'll see you."

"Don't tap on the glass," said Honey.

"We're off," said Fish. "Backaways to Spurn. Lavender's yonder, warming a wall."

They went their way. Issy could feel he was not to be with them. He found Lavender as they said, leaning on a wall.

"Ready, then?" he said.

"What am I doing?" said Issy. "What is he?"

"Don't ask," said Lavender. "If nowt happens you've to know nowt. You can see the right of that."

"Aye," said Issy.

In the truck Lavender opened the engine cover, letting in noise and heat.

Two or three days later again Issy was back in that street, by himself. Jane Ellerby had come marketing and he was with her, instead of Lall, to carry for her. She was buying, not selling. But she had got into gossip with Liz Carnaby, so he left them talking about Lall and Friday. He found his way to the quay, the tenfoots, the street. He came only to look, not to ring. Now in that field had risen a cloth building, not so bright as the stuff Liz Carnaby sold, but greater in quantity. There was some large tent in the grass now, hung on two masts or poles, and on each top was a flag with stars.

Issy looked through the fence, touched the doors, felt he was being watched, and knew it was useless to ring. He knew he needed more help than merely coming and getting in.

A glow of sunshine lit the canvas, and from the front of it there flashed a small extra sun, wiping its heat and light across his eyes.

He looked inside no more, but turned away. Does a wheelwright make lasers too?

Ellerby and Liz Carnaby were still talking when he came back, but he had missed a round of pork pies. Both women looked at him to see whether he had new knowledge. He had none.

About a week later, in a greying afternoon, Laban took Issy down to Stal Ella's knot by the great bridge, through the tunnel of death, and left him with them. Stal was waiting for him, with two of his horses harnessed to a cart. He had no words, but patted the bench he was sitting on. Issy climbed up and sat there. Ahead of the cart he and Stal were on was another, driven by Chowder.

"That Clark's been writing some letters," said Stal. "Birds will have no tails, reckon."

"Didn't send one to me," said Issy.

"Personally he told you," said Stal. He called to the horses, "Up Star, up Star," and they began to pull.

They had a slow journey into town. This time they came from a different direction, and Issy was higher up than when walking, and could stand and see over the fence. Stal pulled at his coat and made him sit down. He had seen nothing but the flags on top of the two poles, poking up beyond the ridge of the long tent, or marquee.

The horses were at the gates. Chowder turned his team in the road, and the two pairs lined up face to face. Stal and Chowder stayed in their driving places.

"Get down and ring," said Stal. "You've been before."

"Shan't be long, then," said Issy.

He rang the bell.

There were footsteps. There was the long looking. Then the bolts slid in their sockets.

It was as it had been before. After the bolts moved the footsteps went away.

"That's all, Stal," said Issy, pushing at the door out of a sort of habit.

This time the door swung away from his hand. This time the bolts had been drawn back, not thrust into their staples.

"Ah," said Stal. "We'll be off, then," and he began backing his cart. Chowder backed his. Stal turned his horses in the thoroughfare, and then led the way down the road.

Issy was left alone, with an open door. He had no one to tell him what he was doing here, what he had come for, and how he should look, what manners he should use, whom for certain he might meet.

He stepped across a high threshold into the field.

XIII

A Sign on the Door

For Lall daylight set the world on its edge. The ceiling above her bed was no longer important, no longer the horizon. That was lying away flat out of the window, and a big tilt had taken place. Lall thought the ceiling nothing like so significant when morning came. She could not fix her thoughts on things out in fields; she could not understand what she had understood the night before. She recollected that she had walked on stone the day before, and then thought she might be under it; but it was all the fancy flavour of dreamstuff: the mind's sugar barrow making fairy floss.

Downstairs, Friday was moving about, lippity lippity, at a comfortable pace, enquiring up the stairs as she passed them whether bacon was wanted.

Lall got up. Her thoughts left all their muddle on the pillow, like a ghost. She knew everything at once, now she was standing. She wanted bacon, and called down for it. She understood again that out in the fields she had been walking on the stone roof of an old-fashioned horsedrawn van, with a raised section along the middle where clerestory windows would be set. It was all clear to her woken mind, in picture if not in word, but there was a difficulty. Why should a van be buried; and who would make one of stone? It was sensible of a sleepy mind to say there were problems. There were.

The morning went by. Friday did not breakfast Lall until ten o'clock or so, and dinner was at twelve, or so. In the gap, today, they went shopping. After dinner, with the day slanting towards its dreamtime again, Lall went to wander in the fields. It was wandering, not going straight to the place she had as her destination. If a dreamy state of mind says something is odd, and a waking state says it is strange, then the thing they are thinking about is somehow unusual. Lall now wanted to know what it was before she got to it.

For her, for people in the coffle, there were things in the rest of the world they had little to do with, so far as the outside world knew. If you do not have a house then you do not have a haunted house. But in fact you have other ghosts, which can be as terrible.

If you do not go to church to be baptized, married, or buried, then the world might think you have no religion. The rest of the world talked about God but never brought him out to show. In the coffle they thought there was something, but never so far as thinking what it might be.

And some coffle people were houseys. Liz Carnaby was a housey of some sort. It was her choice; she chose to choose. Friday was a housey, and she had been made to choose. What others there were Lall did not know.

But out in the fields was something different, she was sure. She knew the flat stones were a roof. She knew the small wall along the centre was a representation of the rooflight of some vans: Jane Ellerby's had a clerestory of just that sort.

It was, however, neither house nor van. It was something else. What?

It was not a house. It was not a van. But there are

other things built. Was it some sort of church for coffle people?

Lall, wandering deep in these thoughts, whether she had them or they had her, was almost run down by the noise of a tractor. She saw it still a field away with Robert Dent driving it, and Edwin Barker walking across towards it. Lall decided, all at once, that she was walking in the wrong fields. She pushed herself through a hedge beside a gate, where the branches did not grow close to a gatepost, and was in the meadow by the lake, where the coffle had camped. The fireplace was a shallow scar in the grass. At Temple Farm a chimney lofted a spout of smoke: there was still fire in the field.

She went across to the house. It was easy to see what room the fire was in. She did not at all want to go into the house, but she wanted to speak to Colin Morton, or exchange words with him; as if he might explain without being asked, and without knowing he had done it, what Lall wanted to know.

She tapped on the window. It seemed quite sensible to her.

"Well?" said Colin, opening it. "There's a door."

"I know," said Lall.

"Did you find it?" said Colin. He was not talking about the door to his house. He was talking either of the roof of stone, or some door (of stone too, probably) that Lall had not yet seen.

"Yes," she said, hoping she did not say too much.

"Good," said Colin, getting ready to shut the window again. He knew; that was enough for him.

Lall went on looking at him. She was thinking, Stop it, don't close the window. But she had no reason to give; she could not ask to know more from him, because she did not know what there was to ask.

Colin stopped closing the window. "We'll go and have a look," he said. "It's something to do with your people, and I've never felt it right to look. But your people never go near it, and I had to tell you how to find it, and I'm sure it's what you want. But I don't know what it is."

"I don't know what it is," said Lall. "It isn't like anything." But her mind, in its dreaming way, even by daylight, was telling her what it might be. She told it to keep quiet. She said to Colin Morton, "I don't think you should tell anyone you know about it."

"I never have," said Colin. "I don't suppose even the Ryan that owns the fields knows about it. It's been there a long time. I believe in your camp..."

"The knot," said Lall.

"...I think it used to be there, over in Goose Hill, not so much in Burton."

"My father is called Gozzle," said Lall. "So he was born there, wasn't he?"

"Where were you born?" said Colin Morton. "What are you called?"

"Lall, and Routh," said Lall. But her third name, the one she told no one, coming to her mind with the others, made her sure, positively certain, that she had found the right field, and the right thing in it. Colin Morton had said it from his own mouth. But she could not tell him. She said, "It's the right place. I know."

Colin Morton climbed out of the window. "We'll go and look."

"Yes," said Lall, standing back as he came through. He pulled the window down again, and they held hands for a moment, in something that was partly a handshake, partly a demonstration of being related to each other, as if they were father and daughter, and partly the signature on an agreement that what they were to do and find was something that only the two of them would remember.

"If you like," said Lall, "you can call me Routh."

"I see," said Colin Morton. "It sounds as if it's the other way round from the rest of the country. But you call me Colin, then, and it's the same thing."

They went across the meadow, and into a field beyond. At the far side of it worked Edwin Barker and Robert Dent. Colin raised a hand to one, Lall to the other, and they passed peaceably by.

"It was never here," said Colin. "Burton Farms are right."

They went past the grounded sailing boats, their shrouds now still with cold and calm. They crossed the bridge and went over the turnips.

"You used to be able to get through round at the end, but the water's risen," said Colin. "Burton Farms mended the sluice to keep the level up all year."

Beyond the turnips sheep lay in a line across the field.

"That's it," said Lall.

"I often saw it," said Colin. "I've seen sheep lying on the warm places, where there's the bottom of a wall left in the ground. So I thought there was a wall here once, and when I walked along it I found the hollow stones."

"Hollow," said Lall. "I did not know they were hollow."

"You wouldn't walk hard enough to hear it," said Colin.

The sheep unzipped themselves from their line as Colin and Lall crossed the grass.

At the flat stones Lall hesitated. "What do you want to do?" said Colin. "Lift a slab?"

"No," said Lall. "No." Because she had then discovered in her mind what this place was, and why it was important. A great many things were not known to her, but about this one she had a strong feeling; and to raise a stone would be wrong. "No one told me anything. I don't think they know how to speak. They think if they know I know."

"I think there's another way in," said Colin. He led her over the stones, and down the slope beyond, where the ground dropped away. "What's it look like?"

"Like a van," said Lall. "The roof. But it isn't. It isn't a van, or a house."

"It might be how your people would build a house long ago," said Colin.

He was pulling away the dry grown grass from the face of the slope, hauling out clumps of roots and earth. He was uncovering a wall of stone. It was not a stone wall, in the sense of being a build of separate stones, like bricks, but what came clear were upright stone slabs, panelling a wall. There were three of them, side by side, making the front of a stone caravan.

Lall came to help. She was hoping the stones would not fall down, because of what might be inside.

"It won't be treasure," said Colin, thinking about the same things at the same time. "But it must be something or it wouldn't sound hollow on top. A space for a purpose."

He hit the upright slabs with his heel. Inside there was a reverberation. Dust fell from the overhang.

Lall broke a fingernail, and bit it off.

"We should have had a shovel," said Colin. "Look, there's a floor under here, another slab of stone."

There was, and their digging suddenly made sense, and completed itself, because they reached floor level across the front of the stone van.

"It's for something," said Colin. "Look, it goes on down further, under the floor," and they bent to look.

"Is there one your side?" said Colin, running his hand on something.

"Yes," said Lall, tearing away at grass. She knew it was right, at any rate, to clear this thing of weeds, to clear the stone wheel she had found at her side, the stone wheel that Colin found at his.

Between the wheels there was stone wall, stone on stone with mortar between, supporting the rest.

"But why?" said Colin. He got up from the ground where he had knelt, and stepped up on to the floor. If this had been a real van he could have sat here to drive it, the horse walking ahead, a door behind him, and Lall as she was now, beside.

"The door," he said. "Shall I look?"

Lall thought Yes and No. She thought Yes because things have to be known. She thought No because she knew. She said neither. She said nothing.

"I can get my fingers in," said Colin. "I can get a hand in. I can shift the slab."

"No need," said Lall, at last, deciding without excitement that enough was known, that she knew what this was. "It's our chief in there, Shemer."

"There won't be anyone in there," said Colin, and the slab shifted under his hands, and weight came on him. "How could there…"

XIV

Nine Bright Shiners

The door dropped back behind Issy's back, shutting out the day he had known, shutting out the street that had been strange to him but made of familiar things. In that street the horses went away, the rolling wheels behind them.

There was no street this side. There stood the dried stems of dead grass, the withered leaves of burdock, the red stems of knotted dock, the skeleton of a tall nettle, kelk tainted with winter; all growing from side to side of the lot.

Down the centre ran the wheeling along which had come a caravan, standing now over to the right. In the track a cold water puddle reflected the universal sky, coming both sides of the fence.

Down at the bottom of the piece of ground something large was set up. It was the marquee, with two poles with soft flags on them, now darkening against a dimming sky.

That was all. No unbolter of gates had come forward. No one spoke. Issy, feeling it the right thing to do, stepped back to the door and slid the bolts over. When he had done it he saw traffic passing in the road, and wished that knocking on the door from this side would let him out again. Of course he could have drawn back the bolts and gone away, but he wished to be told to go, and not have to follow through what he did not understand.

He went to the caravan. It was another trailer, like Jane's, with lace at the windows, steps down from the door, an electric wire to a town pole rather than to a steam engine, a chimney. This one had a doorbell, the illuminated kind, like the one at the outer gate. A wire ran to the fence. Issy thought it was certainly the bell wire.

He rang the bell. The instrument inside croaked. It was what you would get if you pressed a frog. Nothing else happened; no steps came to the door; no one drew back a bolt.

This is what happens, the nothing, thought Issy, when you get to Chimborazo, the Gold Coast, Samarkand. No one comes to the door. There isn't anything at the end, after all. You get there, and that is all there is.

He stood there, having got there, too shy to ring again, too shy to walk away.

That was for a moment. He revived, and thought how Friday would have acted. She once said, "If I don't know the rules I'll have to lick my plate. If they don't like it they can bring me a spoon." Having thought of that, Issy knew that to bring himself to Samarkand was enough for him. He would now leave, and Samarkand could go on without him.

He had a last good press of the frog, put his hand back in his pocket, because it is often cold at the journey's end, and especially so under a grey sky, and went back to the track.

While he had been standing by the van door, the day growing colder and darker, a change had taken place beyond. The marquee, which he had thought of as a thing you don't go visiting at, had changed its nature.

Before it had been a yellow-grey canvas under a blue-grey sky. Now the sky was becoming more bruised above, and the marquee had become distinct in a strange manner. Its ropes and poles, its flags and guys, were black outlines, but the canvas had become lifted from the background. It seemed to be floodlit by something no stronger than glowworms.

Issy looked. A thing is hard to see until you know what you are looking at. You have to be able to imagine it at the same time. Issy felt clearly the distinction between seeing and understanding. Somewhere between seeing and knowing is Samarkand.

However, you are not at Samarkand very long. Behind him, in the road, a street lamp gave a sulky glop, and began to cast a sullen light. The result was that the rest of the world became darker. When it did so Issy understood what was taking place at the marquee. It was merely lit from inside; light shone through the canvas. He had seen the same effect before, at the tent in the woods. In the woods there had already been darkness; here there had been light all round, and at the moment of balance he had been looking but not seeing, seeing but not understanding.

It was clear now that he was to walk down to the marquee. It had been obvious all the time, in fact, but that was another instance of seeing and not knowing what you look at.

Issy walked down there. There was no question of having to lick the plate. He was using the right spoon for the occasion.

As he approached the marquee he found it was casting light on the ground. There were the cut-out shapes of its own ropes against its skin, and there were, at the places it touched the ground, swellings of shadow; and further out, a real shadow where the grown grass and weeds caught the light. It fell on Issy like a kind of warmth, as if his body did not understand what it felt on its skin.

There was a door in the curtain-side, with a ticket-booth beside it. There was a blind down over the booth's opening, but the doorway beside it was open, with a canvas hallway inside. Light diffused through it on two sides and, on the third, plain light was falling on the floor.

Issy stepped in, and turned to the light. He went in a little further, and there was a place ahead of him with a red carpet, pictures on the wall, a sudden look of warm comfort about it. Or he could have gone to the left, into the dark.

He went on, into the warm place. Perhaps, he thought, there is Samarkand, and this will be it. But what he wanted from it he did not know. He did not find out.

He took three or four easy steps towards the carpet, and then rammed hard into something solid. It was as if a door had been slammed against him. It hurt. There was no need now to wonder about the difference between seeing and understanding. He understood that he was hurt, and saw nothing.

He sat on a wooden floor, quietly, but with an echo of a bang in his ears (and the pressure waves of it going round his head, shoulder, arm, knee). He had walked straight into a large sheet of something like glass. He put his hand on it, and felt it flex in an unforgiving way. He could see it now he had understood it, like glass, but not so. It is like that with Samarkand: you can't get through.

He got up. Now he knew he was in some sort of joky trap. It was necessary to look, see, know. He looked first, and hoped to see.

Behind him was the entrance. To the right was the curtain-wall of the marquee. Ahead was the delusive carpeted place; to the left was the uninviting darker district; below was a wooden floor. Above was a lamp, now swinging after his impact with the structure. Beyond that darkness set in again.

Issy rubbed his nose. It was not quite bleeding, he thought. Because of it, because of other bruises, he went cautiously into the darkness.

The darkness was only because of a turn in a passage. It was part of the first joke. Issy wondered how many more there would be, and what he was coming into. He came out into a passage that went either way, and was well-lit, having pictures, he thought, along either side. He knew he was not interested in pictures.

He was interested in these. The first he looked at looked back at him. So much he could tell, because what we look at is eyes. But the rest of the thing in the picture resembled nothing he knew. And then he saw it was moving. Here was a case where part of him understood as soon as he saw, seeking out eyes, being content with that, and the rest was ready to be horrified. It was no picture. It was a tall, distorted, mangled reflection of himself, uncannily tall, a spindly stranger. When he put out his arm to its full length the pathetic monster in the glass put out a slow stub and could do no more.

And does this part of me, he wondered, try to come out from beyond that glass, being thrown back injured time after time? Am I like that, now and then?

The next glass showed him as a globe, more or less, with a moon head separate. And another took the whole head away for ever; and a fourth seemed to do something south-west/north-east to him, blowing him with an optic wind to a diagonal not in nature.

Then he met a bland normal horror, of himself far

away, in proper shape; and after that he saw his own back, which seemed less than possible.

There was a plain glass with a television monitor screen beyond it, and some camera trawled corridors he had not seen, where no one was; until he saw himself, and when he had gazed on that the picture switched, and in those same passages he saw shambling creatures like men with horns, seeking and sniffing, mopping and mowing. A hot and cold sweat walked on his skin; and then he thought comfortingly that he had not heard the monsters within the tent.

When he had thought that, he heard them straight away close at hand, in the wall beyond the mirrors, snuffling, treading, their horns knocking the frames of the passages.

It is not true, he said to himself. He watched the television screen again, and saw himself, and waved, waving back, to prove it. He watched the troupe of monsters take their walk, and then watched all through again. The third time he was sure, and he saw the join in the input, where the screen flickered and there was a change in the quality. The noises, he concluded, were the noises of the frail structure all round him, shifting in unfelt breezes.

He was lost. He had moved round corners in this sequence of crazy mirrors, and was among rights and lefts, now and then seeing himself a hundred times with mirror before and behind; now seeing the top of his head; now himself upside-down on a glistening blister. And the ways out were not there. He would come up against another sheet of glass between him and the place he had been before. He was in a mixture of distortion, plain mirrors, and clear glasses all made into a maze.

Then he came upon mirror-sided steps, and went up

slowly, beside himself, being edged off by his own double as the glass encroached on the treads. Then he came to the top, and walked on a strip of carpet, with wide glass either side. This glass started reflective, and with more mirror overhanging it there was an immense void either side, deeper than depth, going down to places the eye could not see, or mind ever understand.

There was a fading of the mirrors to left and right. They became obscure, dark; there was nothing to be seen through them, and no light on either side. Ahead a slot of light shone on the carpet. Issy walked on with caution, and all the light faded round him, but for the leading bar.

The carpet ended, and the lights all went out. Issy stood still, thinking that immense dizziness might strike him and throw him down space for ever.

Light sprang suddenly out at him, from below, and ahead. Down through glass he saw below, laid out on a couch, face down, a partly-uncovered body.

This is where I die too, thought Issy. But then he saw a hand move, in a stiff wave. It was not at that that he looked; that was not what he saw and understood. What he saw and knew about was the reason for being shown this body.

On its back, at the shoulder, at the waist, and across the buttocks, lay the Nine Bright Shiners, as they were on the baby, a freckled rust on the skin, large, distinct.

"You know who I am," said a voice, as the lights faded again.

"Yes," said Issy.

"I am Shemer Burlington Holderness Wheelwright Orion." And there was full darkness again; sunset on Samarkand, while Issy knew that saying it was meaning it, with meaning not all known to him, though it should be.

When light came again Issy retraced his steps, because that was how he was guided, back along the carpet and down the other side of the mirror on the stairs, and to an exit door.

And there the grey sky had fallen in flakes of snow, covering the grass, eating and reflecting light. As Issy walked away, leaving the first footprints of winter, the light from the marquee faded.

He came to the bolted door, and went out into the whitespread street, under the full vigour of the woken lamp.

He walked to the bus station, having found the chief, having seen the nine stars, his work done.

He got on a bus and bought a ticket to Burton. It was time to go home.

XV

Outside the Glass

Light poured into the stone van. It was not a great light, because clouds were banking up all round. Only overhead was there a hollow place in the sky, not blue, merely empty, a nowhere.

But light did go in.

The light caught first on a stove, at the back of the space. Or perhaps Lall's eyes went first to that, as part of seeing the shape of things. It was inside as it looked from the outside, a living-van, of the small, old, horse-drawn kind. But made of stone, furnished in stone, windowed with stone; and heated cold with stone with a stone-cold stove.

After the stove Lall saw the owners. Then she knew that this place was what she had thought, the third thing, not house, or church, but a tomb. The people were bone, here time out of mind, many years buried.

One lay on a couch. Another sat on a chair, and so much time had gone that thoughts of their being dead did not belong. They were history; perhaps unknown history, but they were so long laid here that they were fossil, as if they had turned to stone. They were journeying still, never being houseys to a grave.

"They are your people," said Colin.

"Yes," said Lall. "I have caught up with them." She was thinking that they were on their last journey, to the last knot. "I think I should not look," she said. "Just to know I have found what I was sent to find."

"This will be the place," said Colin. "I'll put the door back. Will it be any help to you, finding it, finding them?"

"The knot will come," said Lall. "It must be able to."

"You never know, with owners," said Colin. "You sure you want it locked up again?" He tilted the stone slab. "I can hold it on edge as long as you like."

"You can put it back," said Lall. "And if it isn't Burton Farms, then it'll be all right."

"The owner's called Ryan," said Colin. He was walking the slab back into its place.

"Well, you daft devil," said Lall, "then it'll be right, won't it? It must be. It's our land. One of them in there is Shemer Orion."

"Orion?" said Colin. "What do you mean? How do you know?"

"Like the star," said Lall. "Stars." And she searched the sky, bank to bank of cloud, and then the vacancy above. There, laid on the bank of grey nimbus, were the Nine Bright Shiners of Orion. "There, that, them."

"Yes," said Colin. "But what's that got to do with it?"

"Ryan, Orion," said Lall.

"But it might as well be O'Hare, and Great Bear," said Colin. "But I see the stars marked on the door."

"It's our name," said Lall. "Orion." Then she knew she had given all her names, every one, to someone who should not hear them. Lall was enough to give; and she had given Routh from friendship, but she could not give Orion for any reason, and she had. Lall Routh Orion. Her hands came up to cover her face. She had spoken wrong for herself, and unmannerly for others.

But Colin Morton understood, when she looked so guilty. "I don't go round saying people's names," he said. "I shan't use it."

"Well," said Lall, "you knew it already, nearly, if you knew this Mr Ryan in Hull."

"Not Mister," said Colin. "Miss Ryan, I think."

"That's right," said Lall. "Mister is in there, isn't he? It'll be his family, and that's the same as us, and that's what matters." It was her worked-out thought. It was to be found wrong.

Far across the fields the street lamps of Burton were coming on, flaring into the dusk. Out at sea, visible in that large field, a ship's lights came and went. The other side of the lake, that next large field, house lights shone on land and water.

A small dark thing floated against these lights. Snow had begun to fall in the dark, dark itself until lit.

When Lall came back to Friday's house she went straight upstairs and packed her belongings in the plastic bag she had brought them in. She took it downstairs.

"Are you off, then?" said Friday.

"You can stop as long as you want," said Robert Dent, who was warming his feet by the fire. "I've seen Issy, and he's right enough."

"He'll land back when he's found what he finds," said Friday. "He'd better, or I won't have him."

"I've found it too," said Lall. And it came upon her all at once that she had found; she had completed her duty, and no more need be done by her; there was nothing else to do.

"Have you, then?" said Friday.

"I found where the knot goes," said Lall. "Over in those fields."

"The other side, there," said Robert Dent. "There's a

place there, and a well. And there's like a big covered tank."

"It's a van," said Lall. "A stone van. A van made of stone."

"Oh aye," said Robert Dent. "Don't pull this leg, I'm warming it. But pull t'other; it has bells on."

"Take no notice of ignorance," said Friday.

"I saw inside," said Lall. "Shemer's in there, dead and bone."

"Well, no," said Friday, "no, he won't be."

The door opened wide. It had not been hard closed, so it moved gently. Issy came in, equally gently, home from Samarkand, Thrace, Outer Mongolia, and, coming by bus as he had, intermediate stops. He was sprinkled with flakes of snow, like an apparition.

"I found him," he said. "I found Shemer, and he spoke to me."

"Did he?" said Friday. "Him. He spoke?" Friday seemed more puzzled than she need be, Lall thought. Friday went on asking "Him? He?" and clattering dishes on the table. Lall saw that it was simple. Either she was wrong herself, and she had not found Shemer, or Issy was wrong, and had not. But since Issy's Shemer had spoken to him, and Lall's hadn't, and she hoped wouldn't, then Lall herself had only guessed. She had found someone else.

She tried to explain to Friday, but Friday was not listening to that sort of explanation. She had something else on her mind, but did not manage to explain it.

"He spoke to you?" she said to Issy.

"He said he was Shemer Burlington Holderness Wheelwright Orion," said Issy.

"Well, leave that," said Friday. "What's he going to do?"

Issy had come quite in, and stood warming by the

fire. "Give over dripping on me," said Robert Dent. "Have you landed back, then?"

"I've landed," said Issy. "What about her, then?"

"She's off," said Robert Dent. "But you can both stop if you've a mind."

"She can't," said Issy. "There isn't plenty of room. And I've found him, so she doesn't need to go on looking."

"She's found too," said Robert Dent. "Down the next lane and over."

"Not in Burton lands at all," said Issy. "Well, it figures."

"It isn't all," said Friday. "It isn't everything." She was waving a big spoon at the time. "What is Shemer going to do?" and she wagged the spoon, rather than waving it.

"He didn't say," said Issy.

"He didn't say," said Friday. "He. Are you sure that was Shemer? And shift out of the way, Dent, Skirlaugh, I want to get at my potatoes or they'll be pot black."

"It was Shemer," said Issy. "I saw. I saw his back."

"The Nine Bright Shiners?" said Friday, lifting the lid off the potatoes and being covered in a rosy steam from them and the fire.

"I counted," said Issy.

"We should have sent her on that job," said Friday.

"It sounds a bit familiar," said Robert Dent. Lall agreed. It was one thing to look at Selmah's baby's freckled bottom, but a man's bare back and body would be the wrong kind of thing. Lall did not even want to see Colin Morton dressed for swimming.

"You don't know," said Friday. "I was Shemer's mother. But if you don't know what's going to be done, then what is going to be done?"

"I don't know," said Issy. "You weren't there; you

don't know what it was like. It wasn't like being with people, and I just saw through a window. It all came and went. It was strange. You weren't there."

"I'm Shemer's mother," said Friday. "That's what they appointed me. I'd have got more than a name out, I would. Well, it's simple. You know where to go, Skirlaugh. You can go back and find out. And you can take Routh with you. She knows a thing or two as well. As it is, she might frame better than you. Did you say what you wanted? Did you say what the troubles were?"

"Give us some tea, Fride," said Issy.

Lall slept on the couch, her own cabin or van to herself, with the fire purring beside her, closing its eyes as she closed hers. In the early morning something stopped outside, and by first light the door opened and Lavender came in.

Lall woke the fire for him, and they made tea.

"Is he here?" Lavender asked, enquiring for Issy. "We lost him."

"He came on the bus," said Lall.

And it was on the bus that Issy and Lall went later in the day. Lavender could not wait, but went back to the coffle. The truck had bitten a snowy track down the lane, and another one back, colourless, clean.

After the bus journey through a whitened country, the town was dirty. People had trodden the ways grimy and marked the roofs with soot. But there was a cleanness unexpectedly on the heap of junk cars in the scrapyard. And at the doorway further along the fence no one had walked. The door was yet unbolted. Beyond it there was a laid-down patch of ground, the leaves flattened under snow. A movement of wind brought the white winter fruit from the red stalk of dock.

Between van and marquee there was a trodden way.

At the van no smoke rose, no noise came. Issy thought they should not go there first. Instead he led Lall down to the long tent.

The snow had fallen on the roof here, and slid as the canvas sagged a little. Some had slid clear, the rest had cracked into continents. The tops of the poles were pinnacled with snow, and a low sun picked the white into gold.

Under the canvas, when they passed through the door, there was a shadowed light, with a cracked sky overhead.

"Don't go rushing," Issy said. "You can't get through the doorways, they're glass."

But his words were inappropriate, because when they had come into the first canvas hall, and turned right, they were at once in a great open space, vaulted by canvas, with nothing in it but trampled grasses and stalks, like yesterday's field, unlike yesterday's maze of mirrors. All had gone, all had been taken, carpet, delusion, illusion, television, and all.

They walked about in it, warily, and it was so.

Lall was delighted with this living space, the great dry of it. But Issy, when he had paced about, was more practical.

"We must go to the van, and find him," he said. "It's what we came for."

Lall went on being pleased, but for Issy this was but the bones of yesterday, yesterday's man.

XVI

An Assembly of Knots

Yesterday's frog croaked again when Issy pressed the bell of the van. There was no other sound.

"He's dead," said Lall. "I know. I saw." Then she knew she could think better than that. Not all thoughts that come are useful. You choose. She chose again.

She said nothing more, however. Issy rang the frog again. That was his choice.

This time there was movement in the van. For Issy it was the frog waking and walking, long feet lapping the mat. For Lall it was bones coming.

They looked at each other. "I'm thinking daft," said Issy.

"So am I," said Lall. "Bones coming."

"Giant frog," said Issy. And instead of thinking they laughed and blew on their hands.

"Yes," said a voice inside the door. "Who is it?"

"Issy Dent," said Issy.

"Who?" came the question again.

"That's not your name," said Lall.

"Issachar Skirlaugh," said Issy.

"And the others?"

"Lall Routh," said Lall.

"Is that all?"

"There isn't anyone else," said Issy.

"Is that all?" was repeated.

"No," said Lall. "No, it isn't. But who's there? Who are you?"

"Shemer Burlington Holderness Wheelwright," said the voice inside. "And Orion."

"And Orion," said Lall.

"Yes," said Issy. "The same for me as well."

The door was opened then, and a swatch of warm air went visibly upwards into the cold day.

They both stepped in. The entry was narrow, and their host was round the corner of the partition.

"Go easy," said Shemer. "There's tricks."

"Aye," said Issy, remembering how he walked into a transparent but solid wall.

They sat cautiously on a bench beside the stove. Shemer, little and old, sat opposite, and asked, "Whose are ye?"

"Ellerby's," said Lall.

"Friday's," said Issy.

"And what for do you trouble me, these many days? I thought I had lost all these people."

Lall wondered what they were doing here. No helpful thoughts came to her, and she could make none.

"Well, you know," said Issy, but he meant nothing too.

"I might know, or I might not," said Shemer. "Why do you trouble me now?"

"We haven't any Winter Quarters," said Lall.

"One time it was all I had," said Shemer. "Just winter, no more than that; winter alone, all you left me."

"And we got a chief," said Issy. "It's why I came, and you must know or you wouldn't have shown me."

"I'll show her, too," said Shemer. "Better be sure I'm the old chief, even if I have forgotten it myself."

"No," said Lall. "I've seen the baby plenty of times, so it doesn't matter about you. If you show me I shan't look."

"That's for you to decide," said Shemer. "Now, you've looked, Skirlaugh, and I need another witness, choose how, Routh. So Skirlaugh can look out of the window and I'll pull up my shirt. There's no difference between me and the baby but eighty years. Now look, Routh," (as a shirt wound its way up Shemer's back and head) "and see what I never saw for myself."

So Lall looked, as she had to, and saw a pale back, much lighter than the baby's, whose father was Fahkri from Pakistan. On the pale back lay the Nine Bright Shiners, just as they lay on the baby, giant freckles, on shoulder, waist, and low on the hips.

"Right then," said Shemer, with the shirt tucked in again, facing them once more. "You've found me out when you want me. What do you want me for? No one bothered me in fifty year. Fifty year since I went to Burton Winter Quarters."

"They forgot where they should go," said Lall. "They don't know the place any more. We got turned off this year, just when we had a chief as well."

"If you'd known," said Shemer, "you need not trouble me. But it's a life ago, a long life since. My older mothers are dead, and there's only Friday left. However, you know how it was about her, and how she dropped off the Great Wheel, and I paid all. And then they left me to die in my van, over there at Hollym. They never wanted me chief, never, not from the day I was born. Never. Well, they left me, and I left them. But I was still chief, whatever, and it's the chief that owns the land at Burton. So I locked the gate on them, and rented the land out, and it wasn't a big fine deed, but malice. And I went away. I've been round the world, yes."

There was a pause for thought. Issy imagined Cairo, Ceylon, Grand Bahama.

"Weston-Super-Mare," said Shemer. "Bournemouth. Winter Quarters at Cullompton. Then Bridgwater Fair, King's Lynn Mart, Tavistock Goose Fair, Marlborough Mop, the world, and back here to Hessle Lark Fair. I thought nothing of old days. And now you come up."

"We don't know anything about the old days," said Issy.

"No one does," said Lall. "But Friday was your mother."

"She was," said Shemer. "She is."

"She told me," said Lall.

Shemer looked out of the window, down the frozen field to the iced tent. "Well then, be in Winter Quarters this day week, and I'll come and set all right. All that belongs your new chief, and I'll come and forget. And forgive. I can't have a lot of time left for doing that, but I will. So off you go now, Routh, Skirlaugh, and tell them."

They went out of the warm van into the cold once more, and to the gate. Outside it stood Gozzle, Stal, and Fish. Lall did not know them all. Issy did.

Gozzle was on the bike. He took Lall. Stal was on horseback. Fish helped Issy up behind him. Fish walked. As they left the place, Gozzle, in front, slowed down when a bright coat showed in the street. It was Clark Riston, walking to them. Gozzle said a word or two, the words that Lall had given him, of today week. Clark moved on to hear it from Stal, as he passed, and from Fish, as he walked. Then Clark went on, and passed the gate where Shemer lived.

The week was busy. Lall went back to her own van, looking forward as she approached to seeing the baby.

When it came to the point she most wanted to see Jane Ellerby, and talked to her, and talked, and listened, forgetting the baby. The baby had long forgotten her, and cried when she picked it up and called it Babby.

Lall had a fully strange feeling, one of her own thoughts, that she had grown out of real baby as well as one made of sackcloth. She did not need it in the same way. She needed herself, in fact, not it. Or perhaps she had found that she could choose whether to think about it all the time. It was not strange, she concluded. Selmah Beverley quite soon had enough of the baby, each day, and was happy without it for long times. I've grown out of toys, Lall thought. That's all.

All the same, she set to work and re-tamed the baby, several times, and looked into its eyes; and loved it, nearly every time.

The coffle trekked back to Burton three days later, from its low place among the estuary, where all the water had to be brought a mile and the shore smelt of mud, and a distant lighthouse over the water made them feel at sea.

The coffle came to Burton. Lall went in front, on the steam engine, seeking to tell Lavender the way, though he knew it well.

The steam engine turned off down the lane leading to the mere. When they reached the bottom the water lay ahead, and the dry close of stranded boats lay to the right. In the lane stood Robert Dent, beside Edwin Barker, who leaned on the gate to the turnip field, where the notice said the ground was private.

Lavender blew the whistle of the engine. The driving wheels clanked slow on frozen ground and stone. Steam rose distinct and clear-edged in a sunny air.

"It's a bonny day," said Lavender, leaning down in imitation to look at Edwin Barker.

Edwin Barker dropped his cigarette. Smoke hung in his yellowy moustache. He crooked his elbow under the gate and lifted it open, standing it out in the field among the turnips.

"You mind my roots," he said. "Get them shifted. Dent and I are busy, but he'll tell you what."

"That all?" said Lavender. "No fuss?"

"Just come and go," said Edwin Barker. "That's what I've agreed. Dent will show you. Burton Farms drowned the road. We'll let you through this way."

He walked up the lane, past the trailer behind the engine, past the next lorry with Ellerby's trailer, past the rest, to the road.

"Mr Morton came with a note," Robert Dent said to Lavender. "I think we just rent this field, Burton Farms do. But what he says is right, we have to shift the mangolds before you cross."

Lavender sent Lall back to fetch the men, and they came. Gozzle said it was a long time since he'd stolen mangolds to eat. They pulled a way clear across the narrow field.

Lavender unhitched the trailer from the engine, when the work was done, and drove across the bare ground, flattening the clods, and then going straight at the hedge beyond. The long boiler of the engine put the front wheels through to the other side before the back wheels touched the hedge. Young trees sprang up again underneath, and leafless branches whipped at Lavender.

He drove on through, and turned. He had chains with him, and with them the engine pulled the hedge out. The engine flattened the places.

"First fire," said Lavender.

"More important," said Gozzle. "First water. Where's the water?"

They left Gozzle to work on that, and began to bring the coffle through.

In the afternoon there came Fish Swine and Honey Strunch, two wagons and two trailers, Fish grinning, Honey with her urgent eyes and the buttons up and down her coat. The children went furtively looking.

The next morning there came horses, and the wagons of Stal Ella and Chowder Ness.

"Short of running water," said Gozzle. "We've forgotten where it is."

That evening came men walking, Jamaica Kingston and Paul Paull, wheeling their cart.

"Water," they said, "we need water for what we make."

"It's wrong to use the lake," said Gozzle. "Wrong."

"It's big enough," said Paul.

Gozzle was still looking for water, as the coffles came together and set up their separate camps round the field, and solitary vans set up solitary stations, and people afoot came looking for lodging. There were more people than had been together in the memory of anyone.

Then one morning, a week after Issy and Lall had been to Hull, Clark Riston drove in in a large wagon with a living trailer they knew tagged behind it. Shemer had come. And at once all the men of all the coffles began to set up the marquee, driving posts into frozen, snow-shod ground to hold it.

"Water," said Gozzle. "We must have water."

XVII

Shemer's Last Journey

"Well now, little man," said Lavender to Gozzle. "We've got someone who knows things now, so why don't you ask about water, eh?"

"Now look," said Gozzle, "I'm not anyone's boss, I'm not the gaffer. But someone has to find water; someone has to know."

"Give up, both of you," said Jane Ellerby, "Gozzle, Skipsey. There's things we've all forgotten in fifty years. If our parents hadn't been so stupid we might know more. But we can get to know it now, so stand off about the water, Gozzle, and stand off about who runs the place, Skipsey."

"I've plenty to do without that," said Lavender, and went off with the small truck to buy coal for the engine. Laban Gozzle went to help with the marquee.

As the afternoon drew on the field filled up, with people come together but staying a little separate, parking vans and tents, trailer or marquee, suitably apart. There was little room for the original inhabitants, the sheep, who now lived against the hedges, worried and hungry.

Only the middle of the field was empty. No one had camped there, apparently by some instinct. Lall's own feeling matched that, because she knew what was there; but it seemed unlikely that it was all known already. She knew too that when she had found the stone van, and what was in it, she had told no one. And no one had asked. It was as if they knew, Friday, Gozzle, Ellerby; as if they knew and merely wanted confirmation. Since Lall felt that what she had found was natural, she let her thought share itself with other people, like all the other unworked thoughts she had grown up with.

Friday came hobbling to the field, shuffling over the snow. Lall ran to her to walk with her.

"Wintry underfoot, Routh," said Friday. "That's Shemer yonder, is it, the two poles?"

"Yes," said Lall. "He'll be in the trailer."

"Will he?" said Friday. "Well, all these years gone by, I wouldn't know myself if I was Shemer and Shemer me. And I was born his mother, as soon as they saw what I was they made me that. So long ago it sounds daft-like. Where's Issy? Being handy?"

Issy was talking to the baby. The baby now knew him better than it knew Lall.

"Hasn't lost its spots, has it?" said Friday.

"Same face, same spots, same little stinker," said Selmah. "Just waiting for his Da, aren't we, pittler?"

Friday settled by Jane Ellerby's fireside with the door open and watched children bring wood and build a fire on the open ground somewhere in front of the stone van. Near that no one walked, except two sheep, trapped by the tide of vehicles. Stal's children swaggered and waved branches; Fish's looked down and sly, trailing them low.

"I don't recall this," said Friday. "I never quartered here in my memory."

"No," said Jane, "nor I. But it's like old days to have a

knot like this, all these people. All here, I see. There's Liz Carnaby come with her old push bike on three wheels."

"It don't seem like modern days," said Friday. "It's like proper times. Now, Lall, that Issy don't have words when I ask him how it was with Shemer. How was he, eh? How was he like? Shemer I mean, not Issy. I know what Issy's like, I'm his mother; but I don't know what Shemer's like, and I'm his mother too. There isn't no one listening," she added, "that won't understand what I'm saying? Well, Routh."

"He was well," said Lall. "Maybe a bit deaf, didn't hear the bell."

"Fat? Thin?" said Friday. "Dothery, like me, or anything of the sort?"

"Thin," said Lall. "Sort of sharp way, asking and telling, wanting to know."

"That's Shemer," said Friday.

"Wasn't fussed about coming," said Lall. "Didn't want to bother."

"Didn't mention me?" said Friday.

"Said you were the only one left," said Lall.

"Mentioned me by name," said Friday. "Eh? That's right then."

That was all Friday wanted to know. Lall went out and helped to drag wood to that central fire. At the marquee the roof was rising on the poles, lift by lift. Smoke came from the chimney of Shemer's van. Clark Riston came out of its door, his bright feathers like the fire itself emerging. He tucked a writing feather above his ear, and went walking round from little knot to little knot, speaking to the women, spattering his ink as he went, laying down words in a book like a collection of twigs and worms.

The men were at the marquee, with all the noise. Nothing fresh happened until it was up and trimmed taut. Then Lavender ran out an electric line to it, and set lamps glowing within. The front curtain was not put in place on the side facing the field, and there was now a lighted cave. Lavender went back to the engine and set the steam up higher.

Clark Riston was organizing. Now he had everybody coming together round the newly-built fire, not yet lit. He set Jamaica Kingston to pulling it apart and rebuilding it on another site. Lall thought it strange of him at first, since she had seen him tell children where to build. But he was using the stack as a reserve, not burning it all at once. It was going to be a cooking fire, not a bonfire. Paul Paull, because he was the most medical, and Stal, for his strength, had gone into a corner of the field and now brought a dead sheep to be roasted, stolen apparently, and slaughtered.

The fire was lit, with a puff of petrol flame. The carcase was set up near by, because the time was not yet come for that.

Selmah Beverley came out with the baby. By her walked Fahkri, returned from Doncaster and his missionary work for the occasion. He wore a robe, and Selmah wore trousers, so they looked like a reverse couple. Both were smiling. "It is like getting married again," said Fahkri. "It is strange to be having an important child."

"Well, you sit here, and we'll tell you what to do," said Friday. "Next to me." She thought Fahkri very beautiful, Lall knew. Robert Dent said they were all alike to him, turnips breed more different, eh?

The baby gave a wild laugh. "Give up," said Selmah. "This is religion."

The crowd of people began to shape itself. It changed from a full circle by breaking at the part nearer Shemer's van and the marquee. Here it stretched and opened, making a sort of entry, along which Shemer could come.

People waited. The fire flickered. Lavender threw on another branch. Jamaica Kingston went to his tent and brought a handful of leaves, scattering them in the hollows left by the sheep.

Shemer's door opened. Shemer came out briskly, trotted down the steps, and walked up through the lines of men, women, and children, wearing a black coat and a black hat.

"Water?" said Shemer, sharply. "You were always a masterful child, Gozzle, and I remember you was born a wilful babe in this very field, if you don't. Water, is it? Stand back."

The crowd stood back, between the fire and the stone van, at which no one looked.

"That's his nature," said Friday. "Isn't he lovely? And all this time without seeing him."

Shemer stamped on the ground. There was stone under the grass, under the snow.

"This is the well," Shemer said. "Lift this, and dip all you want. You people are without memory."

"We are, Shemer," said Gozzle. "And we don't know that, and we don't know what next, either."

Clark Riston hurried up, with quill and paper. "I know," he said. "I remember."

"Of course you don't, young man," said Shemer. "The last chief you had was eighty years ago, more or less, and I'm the one. And I don't remember. What can you know?"

"It's written down," said Riston. "You just gave me the papers, Shemer."

"I can't read, parrot," said Shemer.

"I'll say, then," said Clark. "First off, are you Shemer Burlington Holderness Wheelwright Orion, chief?"

"I am," said Shemer.

"And will you show the sign?"

"Skirlaugh and Routh saw that," said Shemer. "I won't pull out my shirt for no one these outdoor weathers."

Friday and Ellerby pushed Issy and Lall forward. "Those two," said Shemer. "Right?"

"Right," said Issy.

"And did you see the Nine Bright Shiners?" said Clark.

"Get on, Riston," said Stal Ella. "We know who this is."

"There might be someone who doubts it," said Clark.

"He can stand out here and I'll tell him," said Stal, bigger than all but Chowder, who stood out with him and said he would do the next, if there was one. Then they stood beside Clark and diminished him. Behind them, again, Gozzle and Lavender stuck the sheep to roast, slung on its spit between the iron posts. In the daylight of the dying afternoon, the flames lit the underside more than the sunlight the top.

Clark, like a budgie on Stal's thumb, more or less, went on with matters. What Shemer did was identify the new baby, and make sure it had the Nine Bright Shiners on its back, and then name it. Clark said Shemer should provide the name, but Shemer asked Selmah Beverley for a first name, which was Jered, and Jane Ellerby for the second, which was Rise, where the baby was born.

"Those are purely yours," said Shemer. "Now I give you part of mine, taking it off from me, and name you as well, Holderness, Wheelwright, and I name you that and declare you are a boy and will be a man."

"Of course," said Lall.

"Maybe," said Shemer. "I'm Shemer Burlington,

and chief to nobody, and I'll go my way in peace. It's been a long time since I saw you, Friday. Goodbye."

"Well then, goodbye," said Friday. "I'm your mother no more."

"That's it," said Shemer. "And who's the mother of this one?"

Jane Ellerby pushed Lall forward. "She can be one," she said. "If it'll suit. She's close kin."

Shemer hesitated, and looked at Friday. "I've forgotten your name."

"Tiphany," said Friday. "That's your mother's name."

So Lall was further named Lall Routh Tiphany. No one mentioned Orion, because they were all named that, until all was over, and then, at Clark's instruction, they all said it together, quietly, like a prayer, very secret to themselves and God.

Then Shemer walked across with Stal, away from the fire, through the people, to the stone van. In the silence that there was Shemer said, "My life is over. I go in here now."

Stal lifted down the slab of stone, clear from its place. Inside there was a little electric light, from the engine. There was a chair beside the stone stove. Shemer sat in it, and Stal put the stone back, then came away, rubbing dust from his hands.

"Right," he said, "let's get dancing. Put some wood under that mutton. And what have you got brewed, Kingston? Owt fresh?"

XVIII

Discovery

Laban Gozzle began to dance. He flung off his coat, hung it on a nearby child, swung out his arms, sang out a tune, clicked his fingers, and got up on his toes. His backside began to wriggle, his tongue to tump out a beat. He was not the only one. Nazar Wawne began a snoring sort of humming, and Jane Ellerby put out her elbows and pranced up to Clark Riston, who in turn put out his arms, but Jane was teasing him, and teasing Stal, whom she turned to next, and took Chowder Ness.

"You and me, Routh," said Stal.

"There isn't any music," said Lall.

"I can hear it," said Stal.

But Lall backed away from him, horrified. She could not dance when Shemer had been put to death in that stone van; even less could she dance to a tune only the rest of the world knew. "No, no," she said, dodging to one side and looking for Friday, since her own mother, Ellerby, was afflicted with the heartless frenzy of the dance.

Friday was denied to her. Friday had got up from a snowy couch. First she had calmly had a look at the roasting mutton. Then she had hobbled her way through the loosening ring of people, and caught someone beyond. It was Colin Morton. She brought him back in. When Lall came to her she handed Colin over.

"There," she said, "he'll dance better with you. He's a friend. He can come in our revel and our merry."

"But Friday," said Lall, "what about Shemer?"

"Shemer's gone," said Friday. "You saw, didn't you?"

"But you can't bury him alive," said Lall. "And then go on eating sheep."

"We have," said Friday. "Oh, we have. We have. Now you forget Shemer, and get on with fun. I'll get mine watching, and I'll eat my fill too. Dent must get his own tea tonight, because this is my giddy time."

"I'm no foot at dancing," said Colin, thinking that Lall was shy of showing her poor steps.

"No one knows," said Lall. "Didn't they see him go in and sit down and die?"

"Yes," said Friday. "It's how things are."

Lall shouldered her way through the moving people, to find someone she knew who was still sensible.

Lavender was apart from the rest, with a frown on his face, but when she came to him she saw his trouble was to do with the electricity of a record player.

"I lent it to the mechanical genius Gozzle," he said, "and now it runs just like I should have thought. You'd never think we invented the wheel."

So Lavender was no better than the rest of them.

"Get and see whether that mutton is turning," he said. "You don't seem busy."

"Here's a pretty one," said Fish, as she went by, putting an arm round her, his long face pleased.

"Got to see mutton," she said. Then the turntable started and the music broke out, gearing up all the separate dancers into one cotillon, moving round the fire.

Behind the swinging circle sat the black upright slabs of the stone van, the burial place. In the middle stood Lall, leaning towards the hot end of the spit and giving it a small turn, an inch at a time, while round her the music blared and the dancers stepped careless in the broken snow. And to Lall it was all completely wrong and out of heart, so that she thought that this people she was of must be the cruellest in the world, without feeling to the greatest degree possible.

Then Colin Morton stepped up to her.

"What's the matter?" he said. "I saw you once before beside a fire with tears dropping from you and sizzling in the ashes. Last time they left you suddenly."

"We do," said Lall. "We don't do things. They happen to us."

"What happened this time?" said Colin.

"They buried Shemer alive, and then started dancing," said Lall. "He walked in that van we found, and they'd put a chair, and he sat in it and Stal closed the door, and they began dancing. They forgot him, poor man."

"An abrupt people indeed," said Colin. "Are you quite sure?"

"Yes," said Lall. "I've decided I'm going to marry outside, and be a housey. Oh yes, and not just for a house."

Colin Morton was looking out beyond the dancers. Now the light was falling from the sky, and the fire sent its colour on the stone door, flickering and fading and coming again as people danced between. He said nothing, and stood by Lall, and she snuffled and wiped her nose on her sleeve, and the mutton on the spit dropped fat that flared.

The music ran on and on, twenty minutes or more.

"They gave me another name," said Lall. "Tiphany."

"The mother of the three wise men," said Colin.

"The mother of Jered, the baby," said Lall. "When he grows up he'll get another one younger than me. He'll have to. I'm off. They don't care. They don't."

The music stopped, and there was silence. Somewhere from over the water there seemed to come back a moment's echo. It was not that, though. The noise had come from the stone van.

There was movement there, and light showing. Stal and Chowder ran to it, holding the stone slab that locked Shemer in with the other dead.

"Stop them," Lall shouted. "They're putting him back." But her voice was cracked with crying, and only Colin heard.

He had time to say nothing. Stal and Chowder were lifting the slab down from its place, and laying it aside.

Instead of the small glow of light from one lamp there was now a brilliant radiance of many colours, where a skein of illuminating bulbs had been hung in the roof of the little vault.

By its light could be seen a figure standing. It was Shemer, but changed. The black suit had gone, and the black hat.

"He's different," said Lall.

"He?" said Colin. "It looks like she."

It was like she. It was now a woman standing in the van, dressed in some thick dress of folded or pleated cloth, hanging deep and heavy all round. And her hair was long, though not thick.

There was enough light for the face to be clearly seen. It was the face of Shemer.

There was a shout from the people, a cheer. Stal gave an arm to the woman, helping her down to the ground.

Once more the circle opened, sending out arms, leaving a passage for Shemer to walk along.

And going to meet her was Friday, suddenly breaking into something like a run, and holding out her arms. And Shemer, coming towards her did the same, so that they met and clung together. Shemer, the late chief, in womanly tears and Friday, his late mother, the same.

Lall, watching from the spit, seeing something explained and not explained, felt another rush of different tears. She abandoned her place and ran to Friday.

"Music," shouted Gozzle. "Can't you work that thing, Skipsey?"

Lavender gave a growly shout, about you didn't have to invent the square wheel, did you, and put more music on.

Shemer put up both arms, for a moment's more quiet. The music stopped.

"I've been dead and buried," said Shemer. "You might think I was left fifty years since, but you don't all know. I see Routh here doesn't know; I see Skirlaugh never heard; and I daresay some of you might feel a sort of shame of what happened. But then, I've been about a bit, and I know what funny folk you are, and me with you. Well, I got the Nine Bright Shiners on me, and no one else had, not in more than a hundred and fifty years; me eighty years since, and Gadriel sixty years before that. So then it was me or nothing. But it didn't square with things that I was born just a little girl, not a boy at all. So I started wrong. They had to bring me up as a chief and a boy, against nature. I began as wrong as I could be, but it had to be like that, with folk hoping all the time on a boy being born with the Shiners to take over, which didn't come until now. But fifty years since I had a great recompense to make, along of an accident with Friday, who was my mother then, and it was my own wheel broke, like I'd made it square the way Gozzle does. But my fault, and I paid up. That was the bad sign for all the people of the coffle, and they gave me the bad sign back. They left me in an empty van, like I was dead, just the same as now, and that meant, we don't want you for chief. So I went away. But they got landed with me still another fifty years."

"That's so," said Friday. "We had our ways then, though I don't recall. Our fathers did that, and it's how we had no chief. Shemer didn't die. We did; we died in our hearts and came to nothing. And I look at it now, and I think it daft, because it was just about when the old queen died that Shemer got born chief, and why we couldn't bear a woman chief I don't know."

"But I'm chief no more," said Shemer. "And I come out with another name, giving that old one up. I'll take it from what I come out into, so start up the music, and I'll be Disco, for Discovery, Disco Burlington, and then, Orion," and all the people whispered the name again, and the music drowned it. "And I don't know how I'm in fashion, but this dress of silk kerchiefs was good for my grandmother's best, and I'm wearing it the first time, and I'll dance all night. So let's have music, Lavender."

The dancing moved into the marquee, while the men attended seriously to the cooking of the sheep and the handing round of Kingston's bottles.

As the dancing went on, Shemer, or Disco, made another announcement. She said she was retiring from all activity, and might just live here all the time. When she died in reality, and went back in the chief's burying place, the stone van, then Issy could have her living van. But now, immediately, he could have for his own the Hall of Mirrors and the marquee, to make his living. Skirlaugh might want to get wed one day, she said, which seemed the modern thing to do; and she could find somebody suitable for him. "It was those two came looking and found me. Where you might think of looking for a woman, in a Hall of Mirrors."

All faces and twice as many eyes (except for Issy's) seemed to look at Lall, worse than any Hall of Mirrors. She put her face against Colin's chest, and was laughed at for promoting jealousy.

"Not you," she said. "But a housey."

"Better to be wild," said Colin. "Be wild. We're all houseys. Leave us."

Colin, before he went, and at Friday's bidding, was given by Jane Ellerby a huge teddy bear from the stall prizes; by Fish Swine a pair of tropical fish in a plastic bag (freshwater shark, he said, train them and put them in the mere); by Clark Riston a totally feather hat like rainbows (Clark gave it solemnly, said "I'm sluttered", and collapsed in a corner like a dead bird, ink running from his claws); by Jamaica Kingston and Paul Paull a bottle of their special tonic and another of their brew (which was being drunk by everyone, which meant that everyone was being drunk and getting sluttered like Clark Riston); by Stal Ella and Chowder Ness a chestnut filly (of little value to them because there was no star on its nose, and which became very wild under the lights of the marquee); by Liz Carnaby a bolt end of chenille (enough cloth for one and a half curtains); and by Lall, in memory of when she married out of the coffle, or perhaps didn't, a kiss (not knowing whether she thought it or it thought her); by Friday herself a pickled pig's head (brought by Dent for the feast and hardly started).

And the snow fell; no one was cold, dancing, eating. The new chief watched over all. His real mother and his official mother watched him. He stared himself asleep, full of light at last.